"I promise t

He sensed that Destiny was a woman who kept her promises. And they would be in this together, which was comforting.

"I'll give it a go," he said after a few moments, a ragged sigh slipping past his lips. This was a big deal to him. And hopefully, it would be an incredible milestone for his service-dog training.

"That's great. It'll be an awesome experience." She smiled at him. "At this rate, you might even graduate from the program ahead of time."

He leaned in toward her, feeling playful. "Am I getting high marks from the teacher?"

"So far, you're getting all A's," Destiny quipped. "But if we don't get this lesson started soon, I might have to give you an incomplete."

Luke let out a hearty chuckle. He loved that they were getting closer with every day that passed and rebuilding their old bond.

Maybe, just maybe, he could summon the courage to tell her about the secret he'd been harboring without it all blowing up in his face.

Belle Calhoune is a *New York Times* bestselling author. She grew up in a small town in Massachusetts. Married to her college sweetheart, she is raising two lovely daughters in Connecticut. A dog lover, she has one mini poodle and a black Lab. Writing for the Love Inspired line is a dream come true. Working at home in her pajamas is one of the best perks of the job. Belle enjoys summers in Cape Cod, traveling and reading.

Books by Belle Calhoune

Love Inspired

Serenity Peak

Her Alaskan Return
An Alaskan Blessing
His Secret Alaskan Family
The Soldier's K-9 Companion

Home to Owl Creek

Her Secret Alaskan Family
Alaskan Christmas Redemption
An Alaskan Twin Surprise
Hiding in Alaska
Their Alaskan Past
An Alaskan Christmas Promise

Alaskan Grooms

An Alaskan Wedding
Alaskan Reunion
A Match Made in Alaska
Reunited at Christmas
His Secret Alaskan Heiress
An Alaskan Christmas
Her Alaskan Cowboy

Visit the Author Profile page at LoveInspired.com.

THE SOLDIER'S K-9 COMPANION

BELLE CALHOUNE

LOVE INSPIRED
INSPIRATIONAL ROMANCE

LOVE INSPIRED®
INSPIRATIONAL ROMANCE

Recycling programs for this product may not exist in your area.

ISBN-13: 978-1-335-62103-0

The Soldier's K-9 Companion

Love Inspired
22 Adelaide St. West, 41st Floor
Toronto, Ontario M5H 4E3, Canada
www.LoveInspired.com

Printed in Lithuania

MIX
Paper | Supporting responsible forestry
FSC® C021394

Trigger Warning: This book deals with sensitive content, including PTSD and sexual assault.

I can do all things through Christ
which strengtheneth me.
—*Phillipians* 4:13

For Randy, my true North.

Acknowledgments

For my family who always cheers me on,
especially when I'm on deadline.

Grateful for my agent, Jessica Alvarez,
who is always in my corner.

Thankful for my editor, Katie Gowrie,
who always looks at the big picture and
doles out great advice to make the story stronger.

Special thanks to all the readers
who've asked for more Serenity Peak stories.
There would be no stories if not for you.

Chapter One

Luke Adams gritted his teeth as he navigated his vintage Range Rover along the snowy mountain road. At moments like this, he was grateful that his father had taught him to drive Alaskan roads when he was sixteen years old. If nothing else, he was a pro at making his way over these snow-packed, icy roads. If he could only stop his heart from hammering so wildly within his chest. If only his thoughts would stop racing.

His breathing was choppy as he turned down the road lined with Sitka trees. Luke clenched the steering wheel tightly, counting down the minutes until he reached his destination. How had things come to this point where even driving his truck caused a feeling of panic to crash over him? Not too long ago he'd been an elite Navy Seal, and now he was merely a shadow of his former self. A has-been. A used-to-be.

Lord, please help me find my bearings so I can get back to normal, he prayed.

He wasn't looking for perfection, just progress.

Bent but not broken. His father's voice echoed in his ear, reminding him to hang on. He was worthy of moving on with his life.

Driving was one of the hardest things for him to do now,

which was heartbreaking since he'd always loved the open road and the adventures that awaited him. These days he was always braced for what awaited him around each and every corner.

The red-and-gold sign jumped out at him just as he reached a curve in the road. Destiny's K9 Dog Farm. All are welcome. *Am I really doing this*? he asked himself. His childhood friend, Charlie Johnson, had convinced him to give working with a service dog a chance for his PTSD. So far he'd tried everything else, including therapy. He was still dealing with anxiety and nightmares as well as flashbacks. All he truly wanted was to get back to his old self and the man he used to be. Strong. Confident. Whole. Some days he doubted whether it was possible.

How could it be, when guilt would always hang over him like a dark cloud?

When he parked his vehicle, Luke sucked in a deep breath before exiting. Being in unfamiliar surroundings always did a number on him. The property was beautiful, nestled at the base of the Serenity mountains, which provided a stunning backdrop. A medium-sized home with a wraparound porch sat a hundred feet from the driveway against a lush setting of woods and mountain. Dogs of all varieties were running around in a fenced-in area, looking playful and vibrant.

He noticed a few other vehicles parked in the driveway by the fence. In the distance he spotted a man and a woman with a small dog. Charlie had told him he'd be here, but Luke hadn't spotted his distinctive hunter green truck in the driveway. Now he felt even more awkward about being here, but he couldn't stand around all day without talking to Destiny about her services.

He walked toward the barn, his boots crunching loudly in the snow, before realizing that the woman he'd first spotted must be Destiny. He couldn't tell for sure from this distance, but that appeared to be a training session in progress. As he drew closer, Luke could hear her giving the dog praise and concluding the session with her client.

"I'll see you next week." Her voice rang out as she waved goodbye.

As the man walked past him, he sent Luke a curious glance as if he recognized him. Ever since his return to Serenity Peak he'd been avoiding the townsfolk in an attempt to dodge probing questions about his Navy Seal status. Most people here remembered him from before he went away to serve his country. Naturally, they expected tales of heroism and glory. They often showered him with gratitude and thanks, which he couldn't handle at the moment. Now he couldn't even muster up a single sentence about his time as a Seal without being triggered.

Destiny hadn't noticed him yet. Her back was to him as she focused on her dogs, seemingly in her own world. Curiosity made him wonder if she still looked the same, although it had been years since he'd seen her. So much had happened in his life since those idyllic days.

"Destiny?" he asked as he came within a few feet of her. She turned toward him with a startled expression on her face. "I hope that I'm not intruding."

It took a moment for a look of recognition to pass over her face. "Luke Adams? Is that you? It's been ages since I've seen you." A wide grin took over her face.

"It's been a while," he acknowledged, racking his brain to remember when they had last seen one another. Maybe at his high school graduation ceremony. Little Destiny Johnson was all grown-up now. She was a grown woman and no longer the knock-kneed little girl who had chased after Charlie and their group of friends. With shoulder-length dark hair, chocolate brown eyes and warm brown skin, she was quite the beauty.

"So, how long have you been back?" she asked.

"Almost a year," he told her. Sometimes it felt like an eternity, especially since his panic attacks kept him restricted to his property. Even venturing out today caused him a lot of stress and anxiety.

Destiny's eyes widened. "You must be keeping a low profile. Otherwise the townsfolk would have been dishing about you." The corners of her mouth twitched with merriment, and even though he knew she meant no harm, he was annoyed. He really didn't want anyone in his business or asking prying questions about him.

"You could say that," he admitted in a curt tone. He shifted from one foot to the other, feeling a bit in the hot seat. He wasn't used to small talk anymore, and it showed. Luke was tongue-tied and awkward.

"Charlie told me you might drop by and that you might be interested in a service dog," Destiny said, smoothly shifting gears to business. "Is that right?"

Luke shoved his hands into his front pockets. "Charlie suggested it, pretty much talked me into it if I'm being honest. He thought it was a good idea." He wasn't used to counting on people, needing their help. And now he was right in the thick of things, desperate to improve his situation, even if he had to work with a service dog to do so. It wasn't that he disliked dogs, but he'd never envisioned owning one. Or depending on one.

She frowned. "I'd like to know more. Charlie didn't elaborate about your particular needs. I train service dogs for specific issues, such as for an epileptic having seizures or someone whose vision is compromised."

Charlie was a good guy, a close friend who wouldn't divulge Luke's personal business without permission. He appreciated his friend's discretion. It was difficult for him to broach this topic with people outside his small circle. He'd only talked about his PTSD with his family, close friends and Dr. Banks. It wasn't something he felt comfortable discussing with a person he barely knew, even if he did need her services.

"I'm not being nosy, Luke. If you're in need of a service dog, it's important that I know why. What's going on?"

"I was a Navy Seal," he blurted out, then winced. It was still surreal to talk about his life's work in the past tense.

Destiny nodded. "Yes, I know. I remember all the fanfare when you completed your training. And your folks have always updated the entire town on your achievements over the years. You were also prayed for by the congregation at Serenity Church on numerous occasions."

His chest ached at the mention of his accomplishments. His family had always been so proud of him. And he had lived up to their praise by proudly serving his country. He ached to make them feel that way again rather than continuing to be an object of pity and disappointment. "I appreciate all the prayers," he said. Then as matter-of-factly as he could, he added, "I retired after I was involved in an explosion during a mission in Africa."

"Oh no! That's terrible," she exclaimed. "Were you injured?"

"Not physically, no. But I've been dealing with PTSD in the aftermath," he admitted. "It's stopped me from doing a lot of the things I love to do. I deal with a lot of anxiety. Even driving over here was a challenge." Shame swept over him at the admission. He hated feeling broken, like a weakened version of himself.

"I'm sorry to hear that. Experiencing trauma is difficult, and having PTSD afterward isn't uncommon. I've worked with several clients who suffer from anxiety and stress disorders."

"Really?" he asked. "That's good to know." Sometimes it seemed as if he was the only person in the world dealing with these crippling issues.

Just hearing those words from Destiny caused the tightness in his chest to ease a bit. Knowing that she had dealt with his situation before was comforting. Suddenly, he didn't feel like such an outlier.

Maybe, he thought, Charlie was right. Perhaps there was a way to break free from the shackles that were holding him back.

Destiny Johnson tried her best not to stare at Luke, but it was difficult. He was by far one of the most handsome men she'd ever seen in her twenty-eight years. He'd been a cute kid, but the past decade had given him a serious glow up. With tawny skin, hazel eyes and amazing bone structure, he was a looker. A rugged physique hinted at his Navy Seal days. Luke's eyes radiated sadness, which was a huge departure from his younger years. He and her older brother, Charlie, had been inseparable back then. Luke had been a bubbly and outgoing kid, always full of mischief and fun. From what she remembered, he'd also been quite popular and part of a large friend group.

She was shocked to hear Luke had been home for nearly

a year. Though maybe she shouldn't have been—according to Charlie, Luke didn't get out much these days. She didn't think most of the townsfolk even knew that he was back. Someone who looked like Luke wouldn't go unnoticed by the women in town. All of a sudden she was putting the pieces together. Luke's PTSD was one of the reasons no one had seen him around Serenity Peak. Clearly the poor guy was suffering. She knew firsthand what it felt like to want to hide away from life. Been there, done that.

"So, it sounds as if you're looking for an anxiety service dog," she said.

He clenched his jaw. "Umm, yes I think so. I'm not totally sure, but my goal is to get my former life back. I know that I might continue to struggle with anxious feelings and thoughts, but if a service dog can help me navigate the world around me, then I'm interested." He cleared his throat. "Very interested."

Destiny nodded. "Service dogs can do a lot to help with anxiety. They're great companions. They can help provide a sense of calm, as well as anticipating any type of panic or stress that's building up in a person."

"And they can really do that?" he asked, sounding a bit skeptical.

"Absolutely," she said. Destiny knew why he was questioning the program and its effectiveness. He didn't want to be disappointed if things didn't work out. Also, he was a former Navy Seal. She had no intention of pressing him about the explosion, but she imagined it must have been pretty traumatic to end his career. After all he'd been through, Luke probably thought it seemed like too much of a quick fix that working with a canine could improve his life. And some folks struggled with the idea of leaning on a dog for support. She wasn't sure yet if Luke fell into that category.

"You'll have to put in the hard work and train with a service dog, but if you can do that and open yourself up to having a K9 dog, it will make a world of difference in your life," Destiny explained.

"How long for the training?" he asked. "Weeks? Months?"

"Well, that depends on you. If you can commit to several sessions a week, then the overall training time is less."

"Makes sense," he said, appearing to be deep in thought.

"And if you decide to proceed, I think that I might have the perfect service dog for you. She's already trained to help with anxiety and PTSD, which makes the process a bit easier."

"That would be a blessing," Luke said, the corners of his mouth lifting upward.

Being on the receiving end of Luke's smile made her feel as if she was on the receiving end of a gift. This was how she remembered him—joyful. If it was humanly possible, he looked even more handsome at the moment. She wasn't used to noticing men in this way. For so long now she had steered clear of any man who might be a threat to her peace of mind. She tried to ignore her racing pulse and the fact that she wasn't breathing normally. These were all stress reactions that she had worked on over the past few years. Clearly she still had some work to do.

You're fine, she reminded herself. *Just breathe. Not every man is dangerous.* She needed to respond to Luke in a professional way and not allow the past to swallow her up whole. She'd made so much progress, and she couldn't allow herself to take any backward steps.

This is Luke, she told herself. The one who had fought all of her battles when she was a kid. Although she had never admitted it to a single soul, she'd nursed a crush on him for years. Her sweet protector. She couldn't help but think this was her chance to fight for him.

"Why don't we go meet her?" Destiny asked, motioning him toward the red barn. Focusing on her service dogs always grounded her.

Luke didn't say anything, but he nodded and followed behind her. She barely recognized this person who, as a kid, would talk a mile a minute. The grown-up version of Luke was a bit introverted. Or maybe, she realized, it was due to the trauma he had endured.

The familiar scent of cedar rose to her nostrils as soon as she opened the barn door. It was an aroma she never got tired of. She associated the smell with her K9 business and the dogs she loved so much. They were such a huge part of her world. As soon as they stepped inside, several pups ran toward them. She had four puppies that would soon be training as service dogs. Destiny had to make sure that they were old enough and well suited to be in the program. She also had dogs that were currently working with clients and preparing to go live with them. And then there was Java. Destiny held a special place in her heart for the lovable Alaskan husky.

"This is Java," Destiny said before calling the dog over. Java quickly made her way to them, enthusiastically wagging her tail. "Java, meet Luke."

"Hey, Java," he said, reaching out and patting the husky. At the sound of her name, Java moved closer to Luke and preened as he stroked her. With her ice blue eyes and vibrant black and white fur, she was striking.

"She loves attention," Destiny said with a chuckle. "If she could, Java would stand here all day and let you pat her."

"She seems to have a nice temperament," Luke noted. He dropped onto his haunches, and Java licked his hand. A little smile of pleasure hovered around his lips. It was nice seeing this interaction. Luke was way more relaxed now than when he'd arrived.

"Java is a sweetheart, isn't she? She was paired up with an owner who adored her. Her name was Aurora Banks. You might remember her from when we were kids. Unfortunately, she passed away a few months ago and Java has been back here ever since." She didn't tell him that Java was her favorite of all the pups. At times she was tempted to keep the dog as her own personal pet, but she knew that Java had a purpose—to help others. She couldn't be that selfish.

"That's a shame," Luke said, scrunching up his face. "She was the town librarian for many years if I'm remembering correctly. She used to hold the Sherlock Holmes books for me. Those were my favorites." Luke grinned at her. All of a sudden she could see the boy she used to know.

It was nice to see Luke leaning in to memories from their childhood. "She was one of the nicest women in town," Destiny said. "I was a huge Nancy Drew fan."

"I remember that," Luke said. "You always had your nose in a book."

Destiny chuckled. "When I wasn't trailing behind you and Charlie, trying to tag along on your adventures."

For a moment it seemed as if all the years between then and now melted away. His eyes lit up as if he felt it too. Something hummed in the air around them.

A sudden crunching noise emanating from outside announced the arrival of someone at the property. She glanced at her watch. Destiny wasn't expecting her next client for another half hour, but either her next client had arrived early or it was Charlie. It would make sense for him to stop by to check in on Luke.

When the barn door creaked open, she saw one of her neighbors, along with his faithful companion, Lottie. Thad Josephs was a former client. Lottie, a Labrador retriever, was a service dog who helped him with his diabetes. As a widower and someone dependent on insulin, Thad had been in dire need of a companion after several frightening incidents where his glucose levels had spun out of control.

"Thad," she called out in greeting. "What brings you over here?" She always asked him that question, although she suspected he simply enjoyed the company.

"Just taking Lottie for a walk and I figured we'd pop in and say hello," Thad said, looking over at Luke. "I hope that I'm not interrupting a session—why, Luke! Is that you?" A note of surprise registered in the older man's voice.

Luke's entire body tensed up as soon as his name was mentioned. "Mr. Josephs," he said, turning toward him. "It—it's been a while since we've seen one another."

"I'd heard you were back in town, son, but when I didn't see you, I began to think it wasn't true." Thad reached out and clapped Luke on the shoulder. "How's life as a Navy Seal? I can't wait to hear more stories about your adventures."

Luke resembled a deer caught in the headlights. He opened his mouth but no words came out. "I—I'm sorry. I've got to go," he said, turning around and heading toward the door.

"Luke!" Destiny called out. "Wait. Don't leave."

She wasn't sure Luke even heard her, since he didn't stop

or turn back in her direction. He was walking at a brisk pace toward his Range Rover, beating a fast path away from the barn. Destiny watched the tires of Luke's vehicle churn up snow and slush from the ground as he sped away from her K9 farm.

Chapter Two

What in the world is going on with Luke? Destiny asked herself as she stood in the barn doorway. He had barely spent any time at all with Java or let her know if he was ready to start her training program. She reached down and patted Java on the head. "Sorry about that, girl. I hope he didn't hurt your feelings," she said. Java didn't look put out at all by Luke's disappearing act. She was such a sweet dog, no matter the circumstances.

"Did I do something wrong?" Thad asked. His silver brows were furrowed. "It feels like I chased him away, although I have no clue as to why he took off like that."

"It's not your fault," she reassured the older man. She didn't want him to blame himself for Luke's disappearing act. Clearly, Luke was dealing with a lot of emotions that were bubbling to the surface. His inability to immerse himself in the local community spoke volumes.

"Thanks," he said, shaking his head. "I've known Luke since he was a boy, and the man who just tore out of here didn't seem at all like him."

"He's definitely changed," Destiny responded, unwilling to get into it any further with Thad. It wasn't her place to tell him about Luke's experiences overseas and the trauma he'd suffered as a Navy Seal. Destiny didn't know all of the particulars, but it was obvious that he'd experienced trauma. She easily recognized it because of her own suffering.

Thad shrugged. "Maybe I can connect with him at another time. He's been such a credit to Serenity Peak, as well as his family."

"He certainly has," Destiny said. "Being a Seal is such an honorable profession."

He nodded before saying, "Well, I'm off to meet a friend in town. If you see Luke, please tell him I'd love to sit down with him over coffee for a chat before he heads back." With a wave of his hand, Thad and Lottie sailed through the barn doors.

Destiny gnawed on her lip.

Before he heads back? Clearly Thad had no idea that Luke was no longer a Navy Seal and wouldn't be returning to active duty. Those days were over. He was now a permanent resident of Serenity Peak. It wasn't her place to divulge Luke's personal information to Thad, but surely it couldn't be a secret for much longer in Serenity Peak.

Destiny couldn't stop thinking about Luke's sudden departure. The more she played back the scene in her head, the more convinced she became that Luke had been reacting to being questioned about his Navy Seal exploits. No doubt he was dealing with a lot of issues surrounding his early retirement from a profession he loved. She couldn't imagine all that he was dealing with in the aftermath. She knew all too well the toll trauma took on a person's mental health.

Just then Samantha Law arrived to pick up her service dog, Rebel. Seeing the bond that had developed between the malamute and the sweet young woman caused tears to well up in her eyes. This was what it was all about, she thought. It gave her so much joy to pair up a person in need with a K9 companion who would enrich their lives. The duo was one of Destiny's success stories, and now Rebel was going to live at his new forever home with Samantha.

"I can't thank you enough for everything you've done," Samantha said, sounding emotional. "I've been feeling so much more confident with Rebel in my life. He's become my best buddy." As an epileptic, Samantha now had a service dog who could alert her to impending seizures, bring her medicine and help out in emergency situations.

Destiny leaned in for a hug. "It's been a pleasure to watch your relationship with Rebel blossom. I'm overjoyed that I could even be a small part of this. You and Rebel did all the heavy lifting."

"I'll always be grateful," Samantha said as Destiny walked her and Rebel out to her truck. She handed Samantha a bag filled with goodies for Rebel—toys, snacks, a new collar and a bright blue leash. Destiny vigorously waved goodbye as they drove off. Words couldn't describe what this moment meant to her. All of her hard work in building this program was paying off. This was her vocation in life now, her heartfelt mission.

A few minutes after Samantha left with Rebel, Charlie drove up. When they were younger, people had always mistaken them for twins, until Charlie had shot up like a weed out of nowhere. Tall and broad, Charlie had always been Destiny's protector. His kindness was legendary in their hometown, someone who would go to the ends of the earth to lend a helping hand to anyone who needed one.

But right now as he jumped out of his truck and ran toward her, he was out of breath and seemed a bit frantic.

"Did I miss Luke?" Charlie asked, frowning. "My meeting ran late. I tried to call him but he didn't pick up."

She shook her head solemnly. "Yes, he came and left rather abruptly." Even though she hadn't done anything to cause Luke to leave, Destiny felt as if she'd failed somehow. Luke had come to her place seeking assistance, yet he'd left without getting the pertinent information or signing up for her program. "I was introducing him to Java and showing him around. Everything was going fine until Thad Josephs stopped by, and then Luke couldn't get out of here fast enough.

"Hmm. That's surprising. When we were in school, Mr. Josephs was a mentor to Luke. He was the one who encouraged him to enlist in the first place. He provided recommendations and everything. Other than his parents, he was Luke's biggest supporter."

"Sounds like they were close," Destiny said. "Yet clearly Luke hasn't sought him out since he's been back."

"Yes, they were tight back in the day. I think Luke even kept in touch with him while he was overseas," Charlie explained. "I wonder what made him react that way."

Destiny had a feeling that Luke had gotten it in his head that he had to justify his current status to his mentor. Obviously Thad hadn't heard about Luke's retirement and the change in his circumstances.

"Luke told me about the explosion and his PTSD. I know from personal experience how isolating it can be to deal with trauma. Survivors contend with a lot of guilt and shame." She shrugged. "I'm guessing Luke isn't even sure why he's self-isolating."

Charlie reached out and placed his arm around her. "I know you've come a long way in your own healing. I hope Luke's situation isn't causing any difficulties for you or dredging up painful memories."

Destiny leaned in to the hug. "No more than usual," she answered. "I'm a work in progress."

Her brother narrowed his gaze as he looked at her. "Just remember to be kind to yourself. I know you want to help others, but if it ever becomes too much, I'm here for you. Got it?"

"Got it! I know that I can always count on you, Charlie," she said, feeling grateful for her big brother. He had been by her side ever since the assault that had rocked her world three years ago. She had put in a lot of hours with a therapist and worked incredibly hard to heal from the experience. The last time she had traveled outside of Alaska to visit college friends she'd been victimized by a random stranger. Her entire world had come crashing down in an instant. She had been completely broken, wanting nothing more than to hide away from the world that had betrayed her. She was still working through her PTSD and trying to summon the courage to travel outside of her small Alaskan bubble.

Destiny's K9 Farm had come about in the aftermath of the worst thing that had ever happened to her. Before the assault, Destiny had led a carefree existence, devoid of any darkness. As she dealt with her PTSD, she had begun working with a service dog, Olive, who had transformed her world. Loyal and hardworking, the border collie had helped immeasurably with her stress and anxiety. The service dog had even slept at the foot of Destiny's bed, comforting her when the nightmares came. And for a solid year the bad dreams had plagued her until one day they'd vanished. She owed it all to Olive. Losing her to illness had felt as if the bottom had fallen out of her world all over again. She'd grieved the loss of her dog just as her grandmother, Junie, passed away. Both losses had truly tested her faith and resolve.

But as a result of her own positive experiences with a service dog, she'd experienced a yearning to help others cope with their own challenges, whether physical or mental. Doing so gave her a purpose. This type of work centered her.

As a dog lover, Destiny had taken lessons and worked with a variety of service dogs with the hopes of creating her own business. Her grandfather, Buzz, had allowed her to turn his property into a K9 training farm after she had obtained her certification. She now lived with her grandfather and used the barn and property for her business. So far it was working out well for both of them. Buzz was a proud man who never would have let anyone know he needed help around the house, but thankfully Destiny was able to make his life easier by living with him.

And wasn't that the whole reason she had created her service dog program? To help others? It was so ingrained in her now that she couldn't shake the weight of wanting to lend a helping hand to Luke. Like so many others, he could benefit from a service dog.

"I'm going to pay Luke a visit," Destiny blurted out. "Can you hold down the fort for me while I'm gone?"

"I'm not so sure that's the best idea. He seems to value his solitude these days. Why don't you just let it go?" Charlie shrugged his shoulders. "Maybe he's just not ready."

"Well, he made the first move by coming here. I'm invested in helping him now," Destiny said. "Text me his address."

Charlie sighed and pulled out his phone. Her phone pinged a few seconds later from her back pocket. "I can stay here for a half hour, but I'm meeting a client at Northern Lights this afternoon. Please tread carefully," he said.

"It's all right. I can handle Luke. This isn't my first rodeo," Destiny teased. Charlie should know by now that she was tenacious when it came to her K9 program.

"He's a good friend, so I just want to make sure you don't press him too hard on anything." Charlie grimaced. "Don't make me regret telling him about your K9 farm." Although his voice held a teasing note, Destiny sensed he was serious.

"I'm simply going to finish our appointment, since things ended so abruptly," Destiny said. "He really didn't get a chance to learn about the program. Or sign up."

Her brother let out a groan. "You're really doing this, aren't you?"

She smiled sweetly at him and nodded. "Come on, Java. We're making a house call," Destiny said, slapping her thigh to alert Java that she wanted her to come to her truck. She quickly pulled the door open. Java ran over and jumped inside the vehicle, sitting in the passenger side seat as she normally did.

As Destiny headed toward the location that Charlie had sent to her cell phone, she reminded herself why she was going out of her way to reach out to Luke. Her childhood friend needed help, and it was impossible to ignore that fact. Whenever Charlie's friends had tried to prevent her from tagging along on their adventures as kids, it had always been Luke who stood up for her and insisted she was included. Thanks to him she had built forts, hiked to the top of the Serenity mountains and gone sledding with the older boys. Those moments had been some of the best times of her life.

She had been in his shoes three years ago, and she'd recognized the look of despair emanating from his eyes. Destiny was going to do everything in her power to help pair Luke up with a service dog so his burdens could be lessened. Her childhood pal deserved a spot in her program. She looked over at Java. In her gut she had the feeling that her sweet Alaskan husky might just be the answer to his prayers.

The ride back home provided Luke with ample opportunity to chastise himself for leaving Destiny's K9 dog farm in such an abrupt manner. He was incredibly embarrassed, but he couldn't go back and change things. Running into his old teacher had sent him spiraling downward into a dark place. In high school, Mr. Josephs had mentored Luke and provided him with exemplary recommendations to join the military. He had been encouraging and supportive, always lifting Luke up to the stratosphere.

Having to face him and explain that he was no longer a Navy Seal wasn't something he'd been prepared to do today. He knew that he had let his former teacher down by being unable to continue as a Navy Seal. He banged his fist on the steering wheel. Why was he still so broken? He should be grateful. Unlike two of his Seal buddies, he was alive. His life had been spared.

Yet he still questioned why. Why had God let him live while his friends perished?

Tony Smythe and Rico Martinez had been two of the best men he had ever known. Loyal and patriotic, they had been stellar examples of Navy Seals.

With the exception of Charlie, he didn't have any friends in Serenity Peak anymore, even though he had been born and raised in this small Alaskan town. His folks still lived here, along with his older sister, Rosie, who'd recently moved back from Homer after a painful separation from her husband, Jake. Most days he felt as if he was drowning, between the flashbacks, panic attacks and night tremors. He couldn't even close his eyes without being thrust back into the fiery explosion that had left him with superficial wounds and debilitating PTSD. He had managed to keep his physique in Navy Seal shape, firm in the knowledge that if his mind might not heal any further, he could still keep his body healthy. Luke knew it was a distinct possibility that he would be stuck in this limbo for the rest of his life.

Lord, please make a way for me to heal. I know that I might never be the man I used to be, but I just want to feel like myself again.

He pulled in to his driveway, letting out a huge shudder as he did so. His nerves were shot from the drive. His forehead had broken out in a sweat. Every time Luke got behind the wheel he battled memories of the attack on the Humvee he'd been driving in Cameroon. Although he knew on a rational level that he was safe in Serenity Peak, his mind refused to accept it. Danger lurked around every corner. He was constantly bracing for the worst. His life was in a tailspin.

Other than his renewed relationship with God, the only solace Luke had been able to find was in the act of painting. He found the hobby to be soothing and peaceful. Immersing himself in art plunged him into a world of his own making, one where he wasn't inundated with traumatic memories. He headed straight toward the shed that he had converted into his art studio. As soon as he let himself in, the huge weight on his shoulders began to dissipate.

Luke flipped on the Bluetooth speakers and let music flow over him as he began to work on his latest landscape. "It's beginning to take shape," he said, admiring the bold strokes on the canvas. Despite the events that took place in Cameroon, Luke continued to appreciate Africa's rich beauty. He loved working in different mediums—watercolors, acrylic, oils—and experimenting.

Listening to jazz music and painting soothed his soul. Sometimes he tried to convince himself that these things were all he would ever need, but he knew it wasn't true. He missed being a part of a community. Growing up in Serenity Peak had provided him with a wide social network. As a Navy Seal he'd always had fellowship and camaraderie. Now he spent his days alone.

His body froze up as soon as he heard the crunching sound of tires in his driveway. Who was out there? He focused on his breathing and tried to stay grounded in the here and now.

Hopefully it was Rosie or his parents. He wasn't used to visitors, and he had turned away the few old friends who'd sought him out. Sometimes he felt bad about being such a recluse, but there was no way he could handle social interactions. Even meeting with Destiny earlier had felt awkward, despite the fact that they had been childhood friends.

Curiosity drew him toward the window. He let out a strangled sound at the sight of Destiny and her service dog standing a few feet away. She was looking around with an air of bewilderment. He wondered if she'd gone to his front door and rung the bell. She must have seen his Range Rover sitting in the driveway. Luke groaned. He sensed that she wasn't leaving anytime soon. Even as a kid, she had been plucky and stubborn. That was why he'd always liked her so much.

With a sigh he put his paintbrush down next to his easel. He quickly put his parka on and stepped outside into the cold. There was no avoiding this situation by hiding himself away in his studio. He had the feeling that Destiny wouldn't hesitate to look for him.

Destiny turned toward him the moment the studio door closed behind Luke.

"There you are!" she called out, a note of triumph laced in her voice. "I was beginning to think you were avoiding me." She chuckled.

He walked toward her with his hands buried in his front pockets. "What are you doing here?" he asked as he drew closer, getting right down to business. Luke didn't like unannounced visitors, and that included old childhood acquaintances. He knew he sounded snarky, but he'd had enough socialization for one day. He no longer had the bandwidth to deal with people for very long.

"You left my place so quickly. You really didn't get to meet Java properly or make a decision about being in my program." She was grinning at him, as if what happened earlier was perfectly normal. "I think Java could really be a benefit to your life, Luke. She's a really special girl." Destiny's voice was soothing, and despite his reservations, her words carried great weight with him. Luke sensed that she still had a big heart and a caring nature.

He looked down at Java. She was sitting quietly by Destiny's side and gazing at him with a sweet expression. The husky's blue eyes were mesmerizing. Her black and white coat glistened. "You're a pretty girl, aren't you?" he asked, admiring her striking appearance.

"Yes, and she's one of the best service dogs," Destiny said, pride ringing out in her tone. "I know it might seem strange that I came over unannounced, but I really believe in this program, and from our brief talk earlier, I sensed that reaching out for help isn't easy for you."

Her comment gave him a jolt. It hadn't taken her very long to figure him out.

"It's not," he acknowledged. "I'm used to being the one who helps, not the person in need." He surprised himself by admitting something that seemed like a weakness. Navy Seals were strong, brave and resourceful. Asking someone to throw him a lifeline didn't feel natural.

"I understand," she said. "But at some point in our lives we all need to lean on others. No one is immune, not even a big bad Navy Seal like yourself."

Her words washed over him like a cold bucket of water. No one had spoken to him like this since the explosion had ripped his life apart. Everyone had been tiptoeing around him. So far it hadn't helped him one bit. Maybe he needed Destiny's bluntness.

"Furthermore, it won't cost you a thing. You qualify as a veteran. As long as your doctor signs off, you'll be all set." She locked gazes with him. Her eyes radiated a steely determination. "So, what's it going to be? Are you signing up or not? And if you do, Java's going to be your forever dog. Can you handle that?"

Every instinct was telling him to say no. Just making his way over to Destiny's K9 farm would be nerve-racking. Driving. Social interaction. Becoming a dog owner. It was enough to make his head explode. Yet somehow, Destiny's words felt like a challenge. He'd never been the type of man to back down from one.

"Yes," he said, clenching his hands at his sides. "I'd like to train with Java at your K9 farm."

Chapter Three

Luke's words were music to her ears. She had driven over to his property as a woman on a mission. In reality, she'd stepped out on a limb of faith, hoping and praying that there was still a little bit of the old Luke inside of him. So far she'd seen little glimpses of the Luke she had once known.

She clapped her hands together, resisting the impulse to jump for joy. This was a monumental decision for Luke. Destiny knew what it felt like to be trapped inside of yourself and hesitant to take forward steps. Been there done that. PTSD was a beast.

"Excellent!" she said, grinning at him. She pulled her business card from her pocket and handed it to him. "You can send me all of the forms via email. We can get started as soon as that's settled. How does that sound?"

"Fine," he said, looking over at Java. "I have to be honest. I've never had a dog before." He chewed on his lip. "I don't know a lot about them."

Destiny felt her eyes widening. "Never?" she asked. "Wow, I'm surprised. When we were kids you loved our family dog. I just assumed your future would be filled with them."

"Pongo," he said, his lips twitching with mirth. "He was

an incredible dog. Playful and loyal. I remember he followed you and Charlie everywhere."

"Pongo was the best dog in the world," Destiny said as memories of the chocolate Labrador washed over her. "He was the reason I fell in love with canines. We were fortunate to have him for fourteen years, but I still miss the big guy." She felt a squeezing sensation in her chest. Dogs like Pongo left their paw prints on their owner's hearts. All of her dogs were special, but there would never be another like her first pet.

"So, is it okay that I've never been a dog owner?" Luke asked, shifting from one foot to the other. He was nervous about bringing Java home, she realized. It was slightly humorous that Luke had performed so many heroic actions as a Seal, yet he was afraid of dog ownership.

"As long as you're willing to learn about a dog's needs and wants, you'll be fine. I can give you information on dog food and the name of a local veterinarian. Personally, I think loving your dog goes a long way to keeping them happy." She waved her arm around. "Your property will be perfect for Java. Lots of space for her to run around and you can take her for walks in the woods."

"I bought this place a few years ago." He grimaced. "I always planned to move back to Serenity Peak, but I never imagined it would be under these circumstances. Not being fit for Seal duty stings."

She appreciated the fact that Luke was opening himself up to her, especially since she knew it wasn't easy for him to do so.

Luke's whole life had changed in an instant. He was dealing not only with PTSD but also with the loss of his profession. Becoming a Navy Seal involved discipline and hard work. The dropout rate was high due to the rigors of training. She knew he must be struggling, trying to fill that huge void.

"I hope I'm not overstepping, but did you sustain physical injuries in the blast?" Destiny asked. She knew next to nothing about Luke's situation, despite the fact that he was her brother's best friend. "I only ask to make sure I'm pairing you up with the appropriate service dog."

"I don't mind you asking," he answered. Luke ran a hand over his face and let out a ragged sigh. "Despite my PTSD, I was extremely fortunate. My injuries were very minor. Nothing more than cuts and bruises."

"PTSD can be equally debilitating," Destiny said. Mental health issues wreaked havoc on a person's life. Although her own PTSD had come a long way in the past few years, she still had moments of anxiety and panic. She had only asked Luke about physical limitations to ensure that she paired him up with the appropriate service dog.

Luke didn't say anything in response. He seemed to be in deep listening mode, taking it all in. She was still getting used to this version of Luke—strong and silent.

Suddenly, the quiet was broken by a light blue van pulling up in front of Luke's house. Destiny recognized Luke's sister, Rosie, behind the wheel. Rosie was a few years older than Luke. She used to babysit Destiny when she was in elementary school. Fun and witty, Rosie had a strong personality and an unwillingness to be defined by having multiple sclerosis.

Although Destiny didn't know the exact circumstances, she was aware that Rosie had recently moved back to town after living in Seattle for many years with her husband. As far as she knew, Jake hadn't returned with Rosie. It wasn't any of her business, but she hoped Rosie and Jake hadn't split up. As college sweethearts, they had weathered a lot of storms in their relationship, particularly Rosie's MS diagnosis and a host of accompanying health setbacks that came with it.

For the first time since her arrival, Destiny noticed the ramp leading up to Luke's front door. Clearly he'd installed it so Rosie wouldn't have to navigate stairs. The thoughtful gesture warmed her heart. Luke really was a good guy.

Destiny and Luke watched as Rose exited the van and made her way toward them with the use of a walker. Her body trembled as she moved, which was a part of her condition. With short curly hair and warm brown skin, Rosie was a lovely woman.

"Destiny! It's great to see you," Rosie said as she reached them. Destiny leaned in for a hug, a floral aroma filling her nostrils.

"You always smell like roses," Destiny said as the embrace ended. "It's lovely."

Rosie let out a low-throated chuckle. "One of the benefits of working with flowers. What brings you out here? And who is this cutie?" she asked, reaching down to pat Java on the top of her head. Java appeared to immediately take to Rosie. She nuzzled his face against her palm.

"This is Java," Destiny said. "One of my K9 dogs." Destiny looked over at Luke, waiting for him to explain the situation. She had no intention of spilling the beans about Luke joining her K9 service training program. Clearly, he was a very private man, and although Rosie was family, Destiny wasn't sure if they were close. She sensed Luke didn't trust easily, so it was important that she showed him she could be discreet.

"I'm going to be paired up with Java in Destiny's program. It's time to try and get some help for my PTSD," Luke told his sister. "Destiny believes she can help me."

Rosie's big brown eyes immediately teared up. "Luke! I'm so proud of you. This is a huge step toward healing."

"Please don't cry," Luke pleaded. "You know that's my Kryptonite." He reached out and tightly gripped her shoulder.

"They're joyful tears," Rosie insisted. "I'm happy for you, little bro."

Destiny enjoyed watching the warm interaction between the siblings. Clearly there was a lot of love in this relationship. Luke might gravitate toward solitude, but he wasn't alone. She considered that to be a huge blessing.

"I'm just stopping by for a visit. Do you want to come inside for a cup of tea?" Rosie asked. "Sorry about this guy here," she said, jutting her chin in Luke's direction. "His manners are a little rusty these days."

"Thanks for asking, but I should be heading back to the farm." She turned toward Luke. "Charlie was upset that he missed you earlier. He's going to have a big smile on his face when he finds out you're my newest client."

"He's been a good friend to me," Luke said. "Not sure what I would do without him."

Destiny heard the raw emotion in his voice and saw the way his jaw trembled.

"Okay, Java, it's time to go home. Nice to see you, Rosie. Luke, we can get things started as soon as you fill out that paperwork."

She noticed a slight hesitancy in his reply. "Okay, gotcha," he said. "I'll start looking through the forms later on."

Destiny narrowed her gaze as she looked at him. "Don't

leave me hanging, Luke. Remember how I used to be as a kid? Tough as nails. That hasn't changed much. And now I know where you live."

She wanted to laugh out loud at the way his mouth dropped open in response, but she figured that might ruin her exit line. Destiny turned toward her truck with Java following at her heels. As soon as she settled into the driver's seat she looked in the rearview mirror. Luke had a scowl on his face, while Rosie was laughing up a storm.

"I think I got my point across, Java. Beneath his exterior, Luke is a fine man. And he's going to love working with you." She tousled Java's coat. "What's not to love?"

The farther Destiny drove away from Luke's property, the more she began to wonder if he was going to follow through with his promise to sign up for her program.

She had a niggling feeling that Luke was having second thoughts about his decision. The truth was that she couldn't force his hand. He had to really want to make his PTSD better by training with a skilled service dog. All she could do was pray that Luke followed through.

Destiny wanted the best for Luke. Even though they hadn't been close since their childhood years, she was determined to do whatever it took to help him.

Luke stood in his driveway and watched as Destiny and Java headed down the road and away from him. He shouldn't have been surprised at all by her showing up at his place or the tenacious way she had presented herself. In their younger years she had never once given up on anything or anyone. He had a vague memory of her patching up every broken-winged bird she came across. He frowned, wondering if she viewed him as something damaged she wanted to fix.

You are broken, he reminded himself.

"She's something else, isn't she?" Rosie asked, still chuckling over Destiny's parting words.

"I won't argue with you on that point," Luke muttered. Honestly, he'd been thinking the same thing. Destiny was one impressive woman. He motioned Rosie toward the house. "Come on. It's cold out here. I'll make us some tea."

Rosie followed behind him. "I'll never say no to that."

He made sure to hold the front door open for her to make entry into the house easier. Using the walker gave Rosie mobility, but it was becoming more and more difficult for his sister to navigate the world around her. The symptoms of her MS were getting more severe, and pain management was now an issue. At times she dealt with excruciating nerve pain.

Rosie sat down at the kitchen table while he puttered around and fixed their mugs of tea. A few minutes later he placed the cups down on the table along with a tin of oatmeal cookies, then slid into a chair across from Rosie.

"So what's new?" he asked Rosie. She didn't usually stop by unannounced. With the dissolution of her marriage to her husband, Jake, he worried about her.

Rosie made a face. "Nothing much. I got the divorce papers," she said, her voice trembling. "It's starting to feel real now."

"I'm so sorry, sis." Luke clanked his spoon loudly against his mug. "I can't believe it. The two of you always seemed like end game to me. The perfect couple."

Rosie groaned. "There's no such thing as a perfect marriage, Luke. At the end of the day it's a lot of faith and hard work. We just couldn't make it work."

Luke could tell that Rosie was gutted by the situation despite her attempts to minimize the impact. That was his big sister in a nutshell. She was always putting on a brave face.

"Still, I can't believe he's actually served you with the paperwork," Luke said. "What's wrong with that guy?" He couldn't understand how Jake had made the decision to give up on his marriage. Luke remembered their wedding day and all the promises they'd made to one another. *Till death us do part.*

He looked at Rosie, who was hanging her head and peering down into her mug.

"What is it?" he asked, knowing something was up. The fact that Rosie wasn't making eye contact was a dead giveaway.

"There's nothing wrong with him, Luke. It's all me. Jake wanted us to adopt a baby and I said no." Tears slid down her face. "He wanted to make us a family and I couldn't commit to it. I don't know if I could be a great mother, considering my disability."

Rosie's confession shocked him to his core. Even as a teenager Rosie had always wanted to become a mother one day. When had those dreams dissipated?

"Rosie, your disability doesn't limit your ability to mother a child," Luke said, reaching over and gripping her hand in his. "For what it's worth, I think you'd be a fantastic mom."

"I appreciate that. I should have told you earlier, but I know you've been fighting your own battles. The thought of burdening you with my troubles didn't sit well with me."

Rosie was always in protective big sister mode. Even

before his PTSD, she had always fretted over him like a mother hen.

"Just because I'm a wreck these days doesn't mean I don't want to know what's going on with you," Luke said. "I may not have answers, but I'm a good listener."

"Valid point." She nodded. "I just didn't want you to think poorly of Jake. He's not a bad person. He wanted a child, a family. We just came to a crossroads."

Luke nodded. He knew that Rosie's decisions were always complicated by her MS. He imagined her limitations made her fearful of going down the motherhood road. He couldn't even muster a counterargument, since he knew exactly how she felt. He too had once wanted to settle down and have a house full of kids. Those hopes had died after the explosion. He was no longer the man who harbored dreams like that close to his heart.

What he wouldn't give to alleviate the crippling symptoms of his PTSD. Even now, the thought of attending the training sessions made his heart race at an abnormal pace. He'd become a creature of habit, living his life in a simple, ordinary fashion that was repetitive and predictable. If his Navy Seal buddies could see him now, they wouldn't believe their eyes. He might as well take up knitting and call it a day.

"Are you okay?" Rosie asked. "You're not going to bail on Destiny are you? This program could really change things for you."

"Of course not," he said, sounding way more confident than he felt. "Like she said, she knows where I live." He forced out a brittle laugh. Rosie chuckled along with him.

It felt good to hear Rosie laugh. She rarely did so these days. As of late she'd been as somber as he was, which was concerning for their parents. Rosie was living with them in town until she found a place of her own. Sometimes Luke wondered if she was hoping to patch things up with Jake before she had to make that huge move.

After Rosie left, Luke's thoughts veered back to Destiny and Java. If he moved forward with the service dog training, Java would become his permanent dog. It was a huge responsibility, he realized. But if things went according to plan, Java would be a tremendous asset. From the reading he'd done online, it appeared that dogs like Java served many roles for their owners. She would be a companion for him, one who provided relaxation and comfort during panic attacks. There was evidence that service dogs could even prevent anxiety as well as waking up their owners during night terrors. What he wouldn't give to have some measure of relief from his PTSD.

It will make the world of difference in your life. Those had been Destiny's words earlier today. According to Destiny, there was a clear path forward by participating in her program. She had sounded so certain. So convincing. At this point in his life he needed to believe in something that would propel him forward. Being stuck in this limbo was agonizing.

Could Destiny really help him? She was Susie Sunshine while he was plain old grumpy these days. It was hard to imagine training side by side with her and Java. How was he ever going to make this work? He couldn't match her cheerful energy if his life depended on it. But how could he give up without even trying? That wasn't his nature at all. He'd always been a fighter.

I am never out of the fight. How many times had he and his SEAL team uttered this phrase? He couldn't stop fighting to change his situation. He might not be a SEAL any longer, but he still believed in the Navy Seal creed.

Luke went over to his computer and began to search for the forms he'd discussed with Destiny. He sucked in a deep breath and began filling them out. As a retired veteran with PTSD he had certain benefits that would allow him to be in her training program at no cost to him. It served as a reminder that his many years of service meant something, regardless of how it ended.

Sometimes he didn't feel worthy of getting his life back. Luke was alive and breathing while Rico and Tony had been killed in the attack. The truth gnawed at him. Even though he tried to stuff the knowledge down into a big black hole, he wasn't able to do so.

And he knew that his current issues were linked to his culpability. It had been all his fault. So much suffering and loss, all because of him.

Because of his big mistake, his Navy Seal buddies had lost their lives.

Chapter Four

Destiny was up at the crack of dawn, feeding her dogs and making sure that they were all taken care of before today's training sessions. This was her favorite time of day despite the hectic nature of attending to a group of young pups. As soon as they heard her footsteps in the barn they began making a racket. She swung the barn doors open wide and chuckled as the dogs began racing around the perimeter. The moment she filled their bowls with breakfast they would beat a fast path back inside.

She took a moment to simply breathe in the pristine air as she looked around. The beauty of her surroundings never failed to amaze her. She considered herself fortunate to be able to breathe in clear air and gaze at majestic mountains looming in the distance. Serenity Peak continued to be a blessing. Even in moments when she struggled with anxiety, she tried to remind herself of her good fortune.

She had a full lineup scheduled from morning until late afternoon. Her assistant, Isaac, would be here shortly to start his shift with the dogs. She was so grateful that she'd found someone who loved canines as much as she did. An extra pair of hands at her K9 farm was such a blessing. Surrounding the pups with love was her main focus. These dogs were all spectacular—bright, attentive and loyal. All of her

clients were fortunate to be paired up with a dedicated service dog. Destiny hoped Luke felt that way.

After making sure her dogs were fed and settled, Destiny headed back to the house to make breakfast for her
grandfather. She quickly whipped up an omelet and grits.

When she called out to him that breakfast was ready, he
came into the kitchen with a big smile. "Good morning,
beloved. Something smells wonderful," he gushed. What
she wouldn't give to have his sunny disposition. Although
she tried to project positivity, there were many moments
where she struggled to stay on an even keel. She vowed to
do better, be better. After all, thanks to God's grace she had
woken up this morning. That was something to celebrate.

Buzz made his way over to the kitchen table, his movements labored and much slower than they had been a few
years ago. The extra padding around his middle spoke of
Buzz's love of food. She thought he was the most adorable
man on the planet. Destiny couldn't love him any more
than she already did. He was still struggling to find his
footing after the unexpected passing of her grandmother,
Junie. Although her gran had been ailing for a while, her
death had still been quite a shock.

"Oh, you spoil me," Buzz said as he laid eyes on the
plate in front of him. "You know how much I love my grits
and eggs."

"You deserve to be treated like a king," Destiny said,
bending to place a kiss on his temple. "Enjoy!"

Destiny cleaned up the kitchen and washed her pans as
her grandfather heartily dug into the meal. Her thoughts
veered to the sessions on today's schedule, Luke's in particular. She had the feeling that this process might not be

so straightforward. He had been a bit resistant from the beginning.

"Thanks for breakfast, peanut. It really hit the spot," Buzz said as he wiped his mouth with a napkin before placing it on his empty plate. "So what's on deck for today?" Buzz loved hearing about her clients and the service dogs they were paired up with.

"Well, Luke Adams has his first session this morning with Java." She didn't want to elaborate since Luke's PTSD was his personal business and not hers to disclose.

"Really? His parents told me a few months ago that he was back in town. Jeff briefly explained about what happened overseas so I'm aware of the challenges he's grappling with." He made a tutting sound. "It's such a shame, considering how hard he worked to become a SEAL."

A small sigh of relief slipped past her lips. Now she didn't have to worry about slipping up about Luke's PTSD. "He's not the person you remember, Gramps. Being a SEAL, or maybe having to retire the way he did, has done a number on him. He's suffering from a great deal of anxiety and trauma."

Buzz held up a hand. "Say less, sweetie. I know what it's like to suffer trauma in battle. Of course I wasn't a Navy SEAL, but I did fight for my country in Vietnam. Coming back home with scars of any kind is brutal."

"I knew you'd get it," Destiny said. He was a teddy bear of a man with a big heart. "I better scoot. He'll be here soon."

As she put on her parka and left the house to head toward the barn, she felt a burst of adrenaline flowing through her veins. She was experiencing the same flutter of excitement in her belly that always came along with working with a new client.

"Hey, girly," she called out upon entering the barn and spotting Java sitting quietly by her pallet. The other pups were outside with Isaac. Meanwhile, Java was waiting patiently for her training session. Luke truly was one blessed man to be training with such a sweetheart.

A few minutes ticked by and still no sign of Luke.

He was now officially late, she realized, looking at her watch. She sensed this entire process wasn't going to be easy for him, but she also wasn't going to let him slide if he bailed on the session. This was a business, pure and simple. Sure, Destiny loved helping folks with their needs, but she still needed to pay the bills. Although Luke's sessions were being covered due to his status as a retired SEAL, she didn't feel right about taking money for a no-show.

"Java, have we been stood up?" Destiny asked the husky, who looked back at her with a steady gaze. Why did it seem as if her pups could actually understand her? Or perhaps she'd been spending so much time around them that they seemed almost human. She needed to get out more, which wasn't always easy in a small Alaskan town.

Just when she was beginning to give up hope of seeing Luke, his vehicle pulled into the driveway. The Range Rover's tires made a crunching noise as they drove over the snow. She moved toward the barn's doorway and waited for him to get out of his truck and approach her. Luke's movements were full of power and agility, bearing no outward signs of the trauma he'd sustained overseas. Much like hers, his scars weren't visible to the human eye.

"Sorry I'm late," he said, sounding out of breath as he reached her side. Dressed in faded jeans, a navy parka and Timberland boots, he packed quite a visual punch. Tall, dark and handsome. He had grown up to be a fine-looking man.

Focus on the service training, she reminded herself. *That's what Luke is here for!*

"It's important to be on time for our training sessions," she told him in a clipped tone. Despite the fact that they'd grown up together and he was Charlie's close friend, she still needed to keep things professional. Her schedule was packed, and one client being late threw things off course for the remainder of the day. Not to mention he was cheating himself out of lesson time.

"I know," he said, shifting from one foot to the other. Luke paused for a moment as if he was thinking about what to say. "I wasn't going to admit this, but driving over here was tricky. The explosion in Cameroon happened while I was behind the wheel, so driving isn't a simple task for me. It's actually triggers my anxiety more than anything else." He blew out a breath. "I find myself bracing for the worst every time I navigate around a curve in the road."

She tried her best to mask her shock and horror. No wonder Luke didn't get out much. Getting behind the wheel no doubt caused him to relive a traumatic experience. In order to improve his life, Luke needed to move past this stumbling block. She truly believed that with the help of the most adorable service dog in all of Alaska, he could conquer this issue.

"Thanks for telling me that," Destiny said. "I know it couldn't have been easy."

He shook his head. "Not much is easy these days. It's pretty ironic, considering I thought my SEAL training was the hardest thing I would ever endure."

"Well, hopefully that's all about to change," Destiny said, smiling at him. "So, how are you feeling about training with Java?" The husky's ears perked up at the sound of her name.

"Good, I guess," he said with a little shrug. "I'm grateful for the opportunity."

"Glad to hear it," Destiny said. "Java is in high demand, I'll have you know. She has a lot of fans here in town."

"That doesn't surprise me one bit." Luke smiled broadly, and for a moment she lost her train of thought. Every time she caught a glimpse of the old Luke, her heart skittered a bit. Feeling this way confused her a bit, since it had been years since she'd felt any sort of awareness in regards to a man.

"I went through the forms you emailed to me, but there are a few things I'd like to tell you before we get started. First of all, it's fine for you to interact with Java before we begin. Pat her, talk to her, let her smell you. Your relationship will grow and strengthen with each session. As a service dog, Java will be able to go with you wherever you go. That will be really helpful in public settings. She can help you during a panic attack and can even recognize the onset of one."

"That's really encouraging," Luke said. "I'm impressed." He took a step closer to Java and patted her on the head. Java was the type of pup who loved attention. She began sniffing Luke and licking his hand.

"The two of you are going to get really close pretty fast," Destiny told him. "Lean on her. She'll be a great resource for your PTSD. Not to mention a good buddy."

"I sure hope so," Luke said, grimacing. "If this doesn't pan out, I'm not sure what I'm going to do." It wasn't hard to see the worry etched on Luke's face. She knew how it was to have the weight of the world on one's shoulders. She had been in that awful space herself a few years ago. Destiny was hopeful that with hard work Luke could make amazing progress.

Just hearing Luke's heartfelt words caused a little hitch in her heart. She wanted to help him find his way back more than ever now. Every time one of her clients succeeded, Destiny felt as if the world became a happier place.

She clapped her hands together. "Well, let's get started then. We've got a lot of ground to cover."

Luke's first training session with Java was flowing smoothly. Destiny was efficient and very knowledgeable, and Java wasn't a newbie, so he was the one who was trying to absorb everything. The main thing he learned was that Java's ability not to get distracted was extremely important. Whether they were together in a quiet setting or attending a local event, Java's attention needed to be focused on supporting Luke. Judging by the exercises they did, Java was a consummate professional. So much was riding on his ability to pick things up at a reasonably quick pace.

"Why don't we take a break for a few minutes. You can give Java her snack as a reward for doing so well," Destiny suggested. She handed Luke a small bag full of dog treats. "Positive reinforcement is a great incentive for Java. She lives for that." Destiny chuckled. "As well as her beef jerky dog treats."

"Hey, Java," Luke said, beckoning the husky to his side. "Sit," he commanded, taking out a snack just as soon as Java complied. "Good work, Java," he said, lavishing her with praise while scratching her on her scalp. She preened for a moment, tilting her head up in appreciation.

"She likes you, Luke. That goes a long way in partnering with a service dog. She'll want to help you any way she can," Destiny said with a grin. She was looking approvingly at Java, almost like a proud mama bear.

He'd forgotten how likable Destiny was. She was definitely Miss Sunshine whereas he tended to be a bit grumpy. At least these days he was. He prayed things would change as he found his footing with Java. Luke was beyond frustrated and angry at the turn his life had taken. Not being a SEAL anymore was an actual shock to his system. Most days he asked God why he had been afflicted with PTSD, only to feel ashamed, since his two buddies hadn't survived the blast.

Lord, please allow me to get to a place where I can truly be grateful for all of Your blessings.

There was something about Destiny that was slightly guarded, he realized. It went beyond her simply being professional. She wasn't as open as she'd been as a child or during her teenage years. *Ha!* He was one to talk! They had both changed since their younger years. The explosion had turned his life upside down, transforming him into a person whose life had been taken over by anxiety and fear. Luke didn't know what Destiny had been up to over the past decade, but he suspected she had stories to tell. He felt a deep sense of admiration toward her for having built her own successful business. Luke could only pray that he would be able to forge such a wonderful career path for himself moving forward.

"Would you like a water?" she asked. Despite the brisk

September weather, it had grown warm in the barn after their training session.

He nodded. "I sure would, thanks. This is more intense than I imagined."

She sent him a knowing look. "That's for sure. I also train dogs to work with individuals who suffer from seizures and have out-of-control blood sugar crises. These dogs deal with life-and-death issues. That's why they're called working canines."

Destiny walked over to a small fridge and took two bottled waters out. She handed one to Luke. Their fingers brushed, and a little jolt went through his hand at the contact. Destiny's eyes widened, and she quickly dropped her hand to her side. Clearly, she'd felt it as well.

"Yeah, I know," Destiny said. Her fingers trembled as she opened her water. "People are always surprised at what's involved in the training. It's work, plain and simple."

He took a swig of the water, allowing it to refresh him. "So, what led you to training service dogs? I know you've always been a huge dog lover, but this type of work seems like a calling." He was inquiring with the hope of scratching a little of her surface. So far she'd been the one asking all the questions.

"I wanted to give back," she said. "This type of service training is so impactful. I can't tell you how many people's lives have changed for the better because of it."

He sensed that she was still leaving something out. Although her answer was totally fine, he wondered what her true motivation had been in creating this business. After all, there were so many ways of giving back that didn't include service dogs and individuals with disabilities. Her answer had been perfunctory and lacking in any depth.

"What you're doing here is commendable," Luke told her. And he meant it. Helping people who were at low points in their lives was awe-inspiring and courageous. Just thinking about it made him ache a little. That's what he'd been doing as a SEAL—saving lives and making an impact. He missed doing good in the world. What he wouldn't give to be back in service. At the moment he felt completely untethered, full of uncertainty about what his future would look like. Who was he if he wasn't a soldier? "I know how good it feels to make a difference in the lives of others. There's nothing quite like it in this world."

Soaring. Flying. That was how he'd always felt when he'd been performing his SEAL duties. And he'd always had a sense of being special. He hadn't felt that way in quite some time.

She nodded at him. "I'm sure you do. Over the years Charlie told me many stories about your heroism. There was a really moving one about your team rescuing children at an orphanage."

Luke warmed at the memory of his most meaningful mission. "I've never had a prouder moment in my life," he confided. "Even though I miss being a SEAL, it's nice to be able to remember the missions that went exceptionally well and feel a sense of pride."

"Thank you for your service, Luke," she said, locking eyes with him. "We owe you a debt that can't ever be repaid."

Every time someone expressed gratitude to him about his SEAL service, emotion rose inside of him. At times it was hard for him to feel worthy of such praise. But, for some reason, he was able to let Destiny's kindness wash over him like a healing balm. He hadn't expected to feel a connection with her, but he did. Maybe it was due to their childhood friendship or the fact that she'd dedicated herself to enriching the lives of others. For whatever reason, he was enjoying catching up with her.

"I appreciate you saying so," Luke said, meeting her gaze head-on. He had that charged feeling again. Something rippled in the air between them that he couldn't quite put his finger on.

Connecting with Destiny made him feel conflicting emotions. Because he'd been a bit of a recluse for the past year, a part of him craved social interaction. Yet, at the same time he was wary of opening up to people, afraid that they would get close enough to see what he hid from the inside. In a perfect world, he would pursue a beautiful and caring woman like Destiny. But any romantic relationship would be complicated—for many reasons.

It had been over a year since Luke had been in a relationship. Brenda, his ex-girlfriend, had dumped him after his PTSD diagnosis, telling him that he had too much baggage for her to deal with. *Ouch.* Although he hadn't been in love with her, it still hurt to be dismissed and tossed aside due to something that had been out of his control. To this day, her insensitivity still astounded Luke. She had been utterly lacking in compassion or heart.

Brenda's words were now stuck in his head. *Too much baggage.* At this point it was hard to imagine even being in a relationship. He was terrified of being judged for his disability or seen as less than. Yes, there were certain things about him that were different now, but his heart hadn't changed. And he was trying to get back to the man he'd once been. That was the whole reason he was training with Java.

"Ready to finish the lesson?" Destiny asked, pulling him out of his thoughts.

"Sure thing," he said, placing his water bottle down and moving closer to Java. She really was an exceptional dog. During the break she'd been lying down, only responding to instructions from Destiny and himself. Java was calm, cool and collected, which made her an amazing service dog. Her job was to enable him to stay composed during his panic attacks and lend support. Although it was still early to know for certain, Luke sensed that Java was going to be a wonderful asset. Destiny had been right about the wonderful canine and her abilities.

The realization made him feel happy that he'd chosen to seek help despite his initial reluctance. For the first time in a long time he'd made a decision that could improve his life. All of sudden the huge weight on his shoulders seemed a little lighter. He knew he still had a lot of work to do, but there was a light at the end of the tunnel.

Luke looked over at Destiny and spotted a few pieces of hay in her hair. He moved toward her, lifting a hand as he said, "You've got something stuck—"

Destiny let out a little cry and flinched away. Her eyes widened and her features went slack. No mistaking it, she was looking at him with fear.

"What's wrong? Are you all right?" he asked. "I was just trying to get some hay out of your hair." He had to fight the instinct to try and touch her arm in a gesture of support. Something told him she wouldn't want the contact.

"I—I'm fine," she stammered, backing away from him. "Actually, I think we've covered enough ground for one session." He could see her taking deep breaths. It almost reminded him of the way he'd felt on the drive over as panic took hold of him.

"Okay, then. I'll see you in a few days," he said. "Later, Java." Java responded by licking his hand, which he took as a compliment. The husky was growing on him at a fast rate.

"Bye, Luke," Destiny said, her expression shuttered. Her voice didn't sound as chipper as usual. His mind was whirling with questions, but he wasn't in a position to ask anything so personal. At the moment he was simply her client and nothing more.

A few minutes later he was sitting behind the wheel and racking his brain, trying to figure things out. Everything had been going so well with the training until the sudden shift in Destiny's demeanor. He didn't know exactly what had gone wrong, but he sensed it had something to do with his physical presence.

He ran a hand over his jaw. What in the world had he done to make Destiny react like that?

Chapter Five

Destiny's pulse continued to race until well after Luke left the property. She couldn't stop thinking about what had happened during the session. He'd made a sudden move in her direction, and her body had instantly frozen up. She hadn't been in control of the sudden fear that had taken hold of her. This was the exact reason she wasn't in a relationship. Sometimes the slightest thing set her off. Like the smell of sandalwood aftershave. A deep raspy voice. And, in this instance, a rugged male frame standing way too close to her.

She covered her face with her hands. Destiny was mortified about her reaction to Luke's nearness. There was no way he hadn't noticed her odd behavior. As a trainer, she was supposed to be poised and in control, yet she'd lost her composure. Her body had betrayed her. After all this time, it still wasn't easy for her to be alone in the presence of a man. While her brain told her that Luke wasn't a threat to her, a little voice in her head wouldn't listen. He was bigger and stronger than her, just like Ned had been. She shuddered as the name of her attacker popped into her mind. Normally she refused to allow any thoughts of him to drag her down.

You're safe, she reminded herself. *No one is going to hurt you. Least of all Luke.* It had been simply a reflex and not a reflection of his character in any way. Normally she kept a decent physical distance between herself and anyone of the opposite sex. There were exceptions of course, such as Thad, who was a rather frail older man. Thankfully, this sort of reaction didn't happen very often anymore.

She still had work to do on herself, which was ironic since she spent so much time trying to help others. At moments like this Destiny knew she needed to lean on God. So far, He had never failed her.

Lord, please let me continue to heal. I've come so far, but I still have mountains to climb on this journey.

She managed to get herself together just as her next client pulled up in front of the barn. For the remainder of the day she worked with several clients. The last session was Paige Sampkins and her adorable guide dog, Peaches. Paige was proving to be Destiny's best student to date. Visually impaired, she was making progress at a fast pace with her guide dog, which impressed Destiny and hinted at a wonderful partnership between the two.

"You're doing so well, Paige. I'm thrilled that you'll both be a part of the showcase." She was hosting a showcase at the end of the month, right here at Destiny's K9 farm, that would highlight the service dogs and their owners. She'd conceived the idea as a way to promote the program.

Paige grinned at her. "I'm excited to participate. Spreading the word about your K9 program is important. Not sure where I'd be without your leadership and my sweet Peaches."

Warmth spread through her at the compliment. It was always nice to hear personal testimonials about her K9 farm. At this point in her career, validation was important. It kept her going through difficult times. There were periods in the beginning when money and resources had been an issue. Thankfully, those trials had been short-lived.

"I'm glad we're on the same page. I want folks to understand that service dogs can lend support to a variety of conditions. People don't have to suffer in silence."

"Preach," Paige said, lifting her hands in the air. "I'm happy to be an ambassador."

After Paige's ride picked her and Peaches up, Destiny headed into the house for a quick change and shower before driving into town to meet her friend Poppy for an early dinner at Northern Lights. She'd promised to bring back some food for Buzz, who never said no to seafood.

As she drove into town, her mind veered toward thoughts of Luke. She felt sad that even something as ordinary as driving to a restaurant was overwhelming for him. It must be so incredibly difficult to be limited in that way. Destiny truly believed that by working with Java he was going to be opening up his world. Just the thought of Luke getting his life back sent chills across the back of her neck. The good kind. She would be there every step of the way, cheering him on. After all he'd been through, he deserved nothing less than her full support.

When she walked inside the establishment, a variety of aromas welcomed her. Grilled meat and fresh fish from Kachemak Bay. The tangy scent of fresh lemons and garlic. Her stomach rumbled in response. Work had been so hectic she'd only managed to grab a banana and a protein bar for lunch.

"Destiny!" Poppy's honeyed voice called to her from across the room. She was waving at her from a booth table right next to an old-fashioned jukebox. Smart and beautiful, Poppy had a cheerful disposition that was always comforting.

She quickly walked over and joined Poppy at the table. Her friend stood up and they exchanged a tight hug. "It's been way too long," Destiny said as they let go of one another.

"You look great," Poppy said with a grin. "Loving the outfit."

"Right back atcha. It's nice to get a little dressed up after being in the barn all day with my pups." She dearly loved her canines, but by day's end she was always covered in fur and in need of a shower. Destiny sat down and cracked open her menu, quickly deciding on fresh snapper and a bowl of seafood chowder.

After the waitress came to bring them tall glasses of ice water and take their order, Poppy splayed her hands on the table. Her nails were professionally done in pastel pink tones. At the moment she was wearing a pretty oatmeal-colored sweater and big chunky hoop earrings, a nice contrast to the medical scrubs she normally wore. With her mahogany complexion and braids, she looked amazing.

"So, what's up?" Destiny asked. "How are your patients treating you?" As a local doctor with a thriving practice, Doc Poppy was always in demand.

Poppy chuckled. "Same as always. Busier than ever with all types of ailments—flu, croup and earaches. No complaints here since I'm blessed to do what I love."

"Amen. That's exactly how I feel," Destiny responded. There was something so special about immersing oneself in a profession that brought one joy and contentment. They were both extremely fortunate.

"I heard that Luke Adams is working with you," Poppy said, taking a sip of her water.

Destiny let out a shocked sound. "How did you know that? We just had our first session today." Word sure did travel fast. She hoped the townsfolk weren't gossiping about Luke being back in town and his personal situation. That most certainly would be upsetting for Luke.

"I'm his physician now," Poppy said. "We talked yesterday, and he told me all about the service training."

Of course. In a small town like Serenity Peak it made sense that Luke would seek out the best doctor in town. Poppy had moved to town a few years ago after undergoing difficult circumstances in her personal life.

"I know why he's training with you, Destiny," Poppy said. "I'm fully aware of his PTSD. As you know, I'm a big proponent of programs like yours."

"You've always been very supportive, which I deeply appreciate," Destiny said. Several of her clients had come to her through Poppy's recommendation.

"How was your first session, if I may ask?"

"It was actually good. Luke and Java both worked hard," she said, remembering how well Luke and Java had gelled. Then she wrinkled her nose. "I struggled a bit," she admitted.

"Oh no. What happened?" Poppy asked, her face creased with concern.

"Everything was going well until he made a sudden move in my direction during the lesson," Destiny explained. Shame filled her at the memory. "My entire body froze up," she admitted. "I'm so ashamed that I can't even control my physical reactions. Luke is an upstanding man. He's a hero." It was hard for her to make sense of it all. She'd known Luke all of her life.

As a close friend, Poppy was one of the few people she'd confided in about the assault. From the beginning, her friend had been gentle and supportive, providing a listening ear whenever Destiny had wanted to discuss her feelings or needed a shoulder to cry on.

Just then the waitress returned and placed their food down in front of them. Poppy waited until she'd walked away to speak. "You shouldn't be humiliated by a response that's born out of trauma. Give yourself some grace, Destiny. You've made amazing progress, and that's something to celebrate. And it's okay not to be okay all of the time."

"True," she said, nodding her head. Poppy had given her good food for thought. She had spent so many years stuffing things down instead of feeling the pain. "It's just that it was super awkward afterward, and I wanted him to feel comfortable since it took a little convincing for him to sign up."

"I'm happy to hear it went well," Poppy said. "Luke's a good guy."

"He really is," Destiny said, a smile tugging at her lips. "Have I ever told you that when we were kids he always took up for me? He was my protector. I can see why he became a Navy SEAL."

Poppy sent her a knowing look. "Sounds as if you like him."

Her cheeks flushed. "Well of course I do," she responded, suddenly feeling flustered. "Not in *that* way of course. Just as a friend. A very old pal from childhood."

"Well why not in *that* way?" Poppy asked. "He's kind and loyal, not to mention drop-dead gorgeous. He checks off all the boxes. If he wasn't one of my patients I would definitely be interested." Poppy waggled her eyebrows at her.

Destiny held up her hands. "I'm not looking for a relationship with anyone, no matter how handsome he might be." She shuddered. "I'm still stuck in a place where the thought of it terrifies me. Being romantically involved with someone means you're vulnerable, and I can't go down that road."

"Give yourself grace," Poppy said again, reaching across the table to squeeze her hand. "I'm so sorry for bringing it up. I didn't mean to be insensitive."

"No, you're fine, Poppy. I consider you to be a good friend. Friends can talk about anything. I appreciate you." Poppy had been a lifeline for her during the worst moment in her life. She would never forget it.

"Ditto," Poppy said. "You're an amazing friend too. When I first came to Serenity Peak I was completely at a loss, until you extended your hand in friendship."

Poppy had relocated her medical practice to Serenity Peak after her own personal turmoil, so Destiny knew she empathized with her situation.

They both dug into their meals, and the conversation turned to lighter topics. Even though she tried really hard to distract herself from Luke as they chatted about upcoming town events and a forecasted snowstorm coming their way, thoughts of him wouldn't leave her alone.

Maybe it had been a mistake to provide him with service training. Luke had always held a special place in her heart due to their childhood bond. She wasn't immune to his charms either. Not by a long shot. She had tried to play it off with Poppy by pretending to be indifferent, but Luke's nearness had stirred up feelings inside of her.

And she had no clue how to handle the situation moving forward, since anything more than friendship with Luke was strictly out of the question.

By the time Thursday rolled around, Luke was both excited and nervous about his next training session with Java. If he was being honest, he felt tense about the thought of seeing Destiny again. He prayed that things were better for her today. Luke still had no idea what had been going on with her, but he knew that he hadn't been imagining things. She'd been badly shaken up. A part of him wondered if he'd frightened her somehow, even though that made absolutely no sense. They had known each other all of their lives.

Still, he was eager to get back to training with Java. It was hard for him to admit how wrong he'd been about the program. He had been downright skeptical and reluctant to enroll.

Once again he had trouble behind the wheel as he headed toward the K9 farm. Memories—sharp and searing—hit him as soon as he rounded the first curve in the road. He winced in preparation for the worst. A loud blast sound. Hot, searing flames. Tortured cries from his buddies. His forehead was pooling with sweat by the time he arrived at Destiny's place. With a ragged breath he stepped down from the truck.

"Good morning," Luke said as he walked into the barn. Destiny was standing with Java at her feet, and she was grooming her with a fancy-looking dog brush.

"Morning, Luke. How was the drive over?" Destiny asked. As she brushed the dog's beautiful coat, she looked as if she didn't have a care in the world. It was quite the change from when he'd seen her last. At the moment she projected peace and calm, as well as stunning beauty.

Had he been wrong about the incident during the previous session? He didn't think so, but he knew it was for the best to push it to the back of his mind. He'd asked her at the time what was wrong, and she'd said she was fine. It would be odd if he brought up the incident now.

"Pretty rough if I'm being honest," Luke told her. It wasn't easy admitting his human frailties, particularly since it involved something he'd learned to do at sixteen years old. Driving had always given him such freedom and autonomy. Now it was unpredictable, and at times, terror inducing.

"Okay," she said with a nod. "You've done it your way so far, but now I'm going to make a suggestion."

"Uh-oh. You sound serious," Luke said, shifting from one foot to the other. He had the feeling that she was about to throw him a curveball.

"Don't worry," she said, chuckling. "This will be an easy fix. Take Java home with you. She's trained to deal with anxiety and panic. If the ride home is problematic, she'll help you through it. It can totally be a game changer."

He frowned. "So would she stay over? And I would be responsible for her?" The thought of taking care of Java so soon threw him for a loop. He'd never had his own dog before and never cared for one. Was he up to the task?

"Yes, and you could bring her back with you when you have your next lesson."

"I'm not sure if I'm ready to keep Java overnight. I need more time." Even as the words came out of his mouth, he knew they sounded ridiculous. Java was a low-maintenance dog who didn't need much.

She reached out and lightly touched his arm. "Java is trained to provide comfort during anxiety attacks. If she's with you in the vehicle, her presence can provide a calming effect. And in your paperwork you indicated that you suffer from night terrors. She can assist you in that area as well."

"I'm not sure that I'm equipped to care for her needs overnight. I—I don't have bedding or food for Java at my place." Now he was floundering, trying to find reasons and failing miserably. All he knew was that it seemed as if Destiny was expecting way more from him than he could give at this stage. She was pushing him to do something he didn't think he was ready for. And now, as a result, he was being forced to come up with reasons not to take Java home with him.

Destiny arched an eyebrow at him and placed her hand on her hip. "I can supply her food for you. Making sure she's hydrated and taking her outside to do her business are the only other duties. Treat her lovingly and with care. It's very straightforward." The look she gave him almost challenged him to dispute what she'd said.

He didn't have a single reason to say no, and he knew it. So he nodded his head. "I'll give it a try," he said. "I'll take her home with me." So far Destiny had been spot-on regarding everything she'd told him about Java. He wasn't going to start doubting her now.

Destiny seemed to be elated by his willingness to bring Java home. The huge smile that lit up her face caused a hitch in the center of his heart. It was nice to know he could still make her grin as he'd done in their younger years.

Easy there, he reminded himself. Destiny was a friend

and nothing more. And that was where their relationship needed to stay.

Even if he wanted her to be something more, there were mountains standing between them. She was Charlie's kid sister for starters. He had no idea how Charlie would feel if something developed between them. Secondly, he was Destiny's client, and his focus should be on training with Java.

Most importantly, he couldn't afford for Destiny to get close to him. He didn't want anyone to know that he was responsible for Tony's and Rico's deaths. Luke could only imagine Destiny's horror and disgust if she ever found out.

"On that note, let's get started. I want to focus today on Java responding to your commands. She's already well trained in this area but with another handler. This exercise will reinforce that you're the one who'll be giving her the commands from this point on. It'll show you just what she can do."

"Let's do this!" Luke said, feeling energized by the assignment. He couldn't believe how quickly Destiny and Java had made a believer out of him. The fact that his life might get better due to an Alaskan husky and service training was a bit mind blowing. In the best way of course.

Destiny put them both through their paces for the next forty-five minutes, with Java showcasing her top-notch skills. Java could fetch medicine, lead him toward an exit during a panic attack, keep people from approaching him and ground him during an episode, as well as performing many other duties.

"What a good girl you are," Luke crooned as he lavished the canine with praise.

"Don't forget her treat. It's great positive reinforcement," Destiny said, handing him a dog biscuit. He got down on his haunches and met Java eye to eye. She really was a wonderful pup. Next thing he knew Destiny was beside him, rubbing Java's back.

"We might be spoiling her with all this attention."

"She deserves it," Luke said, meeting Destiny's gaze while continuing to pat Java.

They were so close to one another that Luke could spot the caramel flecks in her brown eyes and the tiny freckles on the bridge of her nose. He could hear her shallow breaths. His own heart was beating a wild rhythm in his chest.

One slight move in her direction and their lips would be practically touching.

A sharp knocking followed by the creaking sound of the barn door opening broke the moment, catching them both off guard. Destiny's grandfather was standing in the entryway, taking tentative steps toward them. Buzz, wearing faded overalls and a chunky cardigan sweater, had a pleasant expression on his face.

"I hope I'm not interrupting. I couldn't resist the opportunity to see one of my favorite people. It's been a long time, Luke."

"Buzz!" Luke said, joy rising up inside of him at the sight of the older man. He could feel a smile stretching across his face. Warm and caring, Buzz had always given him a firm shoulder to lean on. The doors of his home had always been wide-open and welcoming.

Luke walked toward him, meeting Buzz halfway. They exchanged a hearty hug that exuded mutual affection.

"It's so good to see you," Luke said, clapping him on the shoulder.

"You as well. I have such good memories of you and

Charlie running around Serenity Peak as thick as thieves." Buzz chuckled. "The two of you were inseparable."

Luke's childhood in Serenity Peak had been full of wonder and adventure. He couldn't imagine growing up anywhere else but Alaska.

"I was sorry to hear about Mrs. Junie." Destiny and Charlie's grandmother had been an amazing woman of faith. Wife. Mother. Friend.

Buzz blinked back tears. "Losing Junie was a heartbreak. She was a good woman. Fifty-five years of marriage. And it still wasn't enough."

Destiny put her arm around her grandfather and nestled against his side. "No, it wasn't, was it? But you made her so happy. The two of you will forever be my benchmark."

Buzz gripped her hand. "My wish for you is that you find a similar type of love. Enduring and true. A vow keeper."

Just watching their interaction caused a groundswell of emotion that choked him up. The Johnsons had always been a beautiful, down-to-earth family. He had always envied the fact that Charlie and Destiny had a solid foundation that he'd never really had with his own family. If he was ever blessed to have a family of his own, this would be the goal. Closeness and unity.

"Well, I didn't want to mess up your lesson, but I made some of my special Bolognese sauce and you're welcome to come inside and partake of it once you've finished up in here, Luke," Buzz said.

His invitation was enticing. Luke remembered that he was a great cook and it had been ages since he'd sat down at Buzz's table. Destiny must have seen the eager expression on his face since she grinned at him.

"We're almost done here, so we'll come up to the house

soon. Isaac is taking the next training session," Destiny explained. With a wave of his hand, Buzz exited the barn just as discreetly as he'd made his entrance.

Destiny must have seen the eager expression on his face since she grinned at him as soon as Buzz left. "Want to call it a day? It's been a great session." She glanced at her watch. "Five minutes won't matter much."

Luke playfully rubbed his tummy. "If you insist."

Destiny let out a low chuckle. "Come on. Let's go. I have something to tell you about on the walk over."

"Okay," Luke said. "I'm all ears."

As they walked Destiny began talking. "I'm hosting a K9 showcase here at the farm, and I'm asking all of my clients if they're interested in participating. I would like you to be a part of it."

Him? In a canine showcase? He wasn't sure that he could pull off something like that without falling on his face. He didn't trust himself enough at the moment. And the very last thing he wanted to do was let Destiny down. The thought of disappointing her filled him with a sense of dread. "I don't know if I can add anything to the program. I'm pretty new at this." The last thing he wanted to do was mess up her program or fall on his face.

"My goal is to have handlers who are at all levels in their service dog journey. With the progress you've been making, I think you would be a stellar participant."

Being praised by Destiny felt good. As of late he didn't get much of it. In the past Luke had always received words of positivity from his various SEAL commanders. That encouragement had spurred him on to do better, be better. He had been a textbook example of a successful Navy

SEAL—strong, brave and loyal. The best of the best. Just thinking about it reinforced how much he'd lost.

"When is it taking place?" he asked. Maybe this would be good for him. The event would make him train harder with Java and serve as an inspiration to stay on track.

"Roughly in four weeks. I still have to pick a firm date."

He surprised himself by jumping right in. "I think I'd like to do it. Folks should see how wonderful Java is." And Destiny. He should have added that she was a huge draw.

"The two of you make a great team." She bit her lip. "I should mention that the showcase would place you right in the spotlight. I don't know if that's going to work for you, since you've been a bit reclusive since you've been back home."

Home. That was exactly why he'd come back to Serenity Peak. To lick his wounds and heal in a place that was meaningful to him. And now he was finally making progress thanks to Destiny and Java. A big part of him wanted to show Destiny that her faith in him hadn't been misplaced.

"I'm working toward coming out of my little bubble," Luke said. "Coming here has been helping me a lot in so many ways."

A sigh slipped past his lips. He knew it was time to reclaim his life, and one of the best ways to do so was to become a part of the local community. Charlie and Rosie had been encouraging him to do so for months now. Up until now he hadn't felt ready. Doing the showcase would be good for him. Meeting Mr. Josephs for coffee would also be a huge step forward. At some point he needed to reach out to his local friends.

"I'm happy to hear that. Your name is going at the top of my showcase list," Destiny said as she pulled open the front door of the house. The moment Luke stepped inside the house, the heady aroma of sauce assailed his senses.

Being in Buzz's kitchen felt like old times. As a child, he'd sat at this table with the Johnson family and eaten spaghetti and meatballs until his belly ached. He had loved those moments of connection, especially since his own home hadn't been as joyful. His parents had loved him and Rosie, but they had never put their children first.

"Chicken parm," Luke said when Buzz laid their plates down in front of them. He rubbed his hands together. "What a treat."

"I hope you still love it as much as you used to," Buzz said, his gaze trained on Luke.

"It would seem so, judging by the fact that Luke is practically salivating," Destiny teased.

Luke laughed along with Buzz. It was amazing how quickly they had all slipped into old rhythms. He felt comfortable in this home and with these old friends in a way he hadn't felt since he'd been back in Serenity Peak.

"Destiny insists on making most of my meals for me, but I still like the adventure of cooking," Buzz said. "It keeps me young at heart." He winked at Luke.

Buzz was right. Everyone had a passion that enhanced their life. These days Luke immersed himself in painting as a way to be creative and work through his anxiety. He imagined that working with canines filled that need in Destiny.

"Let's say grace before we dig in," Destiny said, reaching out for his and Buzz's hands. He joined hands with Destiny and Buzz, then bowed his head to pray over the food. At this moment he felt settled. Luke had been praying for a solid year for things to get better. And now they were finally looking up. He was a long way from being healed, but instead of seeing shadows all the time, he now saw rays of light.

As he dug into the meal, his thoughts wandered. Luke couldn't help but wonder what might have happened between him and Destiny if Buzz hadn't interrupted them in the barn.

Chapter Six

Destiny saw Luke and Java off, waving at them as Luke drove away with the pup in the passenger seat. She watched as they rounded the bend in the road and disappeared from view. She prayed that the special canine's presence would ease Luke's anxiety and bring him a step closer to healing. After all he'd given for his country, Luke deserved a little peace.

Lord, please use Java as Your vessel to give Luke freedom from panic and anxiety. Help him heal.

"Penny for your thoughts." Her grandfather's raspy voice murmured by her ear. Buzz had silently crept up behind her as she stood in the doorway.

"Not sure if they're worth that," she quipped. Her grandfather might be shocked at the tender thoughts Luke had inspired. It had been years since she had been romantically interested in anyone. Ever since the assault, Destiny had wanted nothing to do with dating. She had completely shut down that part of her life. Destiny no longer wanted to put herself out there. The risk of being hurt felt too high.

"I find that hard to believe. You've always been a deep thinker." She felt Buzz's hand on her shoulder. "I know something happened that took the sparkle out of your eyes. I'm happy to see you bouncing back."

Tears moistened her eyes and she blinked them away. She willed herself not to break down. "I never wanted to burden you with my problems."

How could she ever have summoned the courage to tell him something so shocking? She hadn't even told her parents, who had been traveling all over the world since their retirement and were rarely in town. Revealing something so devastating had seemed daunting to Destiny. It had been difficult enough for her to process the assault herself, let alone share the news with her family.

"You're a large piece of my heart," Buzz said. "There's nothing too big for you to place on my shoulders. I can handle it." He winked at her. "I'm a decorated Vietnam veteran, I'll have you know."

She nestled herself against his side. "And I'm very proud of all your accomplishments. You rock."

"That's a good thing, right?" he asked, his brow furrowed.

Destiny nodded. "Absolutely. The very best."

For a moment Buzz seemed to be studying her. "I sensed something brewing between you and Luke," he said. "A connection. Am I right?"

"We're just friends," she responded quickly. "Always have been." The last thing she wanted to do was encourage her grandfather to play matchmaker. He was a romantic at heart, and she knew that he loved to see couples paired up.

"That's how it started between your grandmother and me," he said, his eyes twinkling.

She chuckled. Her sweet grandfather was too funny sometimes. She was just relieved to see him smiling and happy. Grieving his wife had been a brutal process.

"I better get back at it," she said, pressing a kiss against his cheek. "Thanks for lunch."

On the walk back to the barn, Destiny took a moment to wander across the property. Last night's snow had left them with a few inches of the fluffy white stuff. She breathed in the pristine air. Being in Alaska grounded her. It had always been a refuge from the storms of life.

She'd come so far in the past three years. Destiny knew that with a deep certainty. Yet she also realized that she still had miles to go on her journey. Freezing up when Luke made a sudden move in her direction still gnawed at her. But, unlike past instances with other men, she'd never truly believed that Luke would hurt her. That was definitely something to hold on to. And she had reached out and touched his arm earlier. She wouldn't have done that if she didn't trust him.

Destiny knew why she was still in limbo. She still blamed herself for the assault. The circumstances continued to nag at her. Why had she ever agreed to go on a date with Ned Timmons? She should have stuck with her friends on their Nashville girls trip rather than agreeing to go on a date. Ned had seemed so harmless, until he wasn't. Destiny had been in such shock that she hadn't filed charges. To this day, Charlie and Poppy were the only ones she had confided in. Even though Luke inspired her to step out on a limb of faith, fear was ever present. She was afraid of confronting the past and being judged for what had happened.

Here she was encouraging Luke to go outside of his comfort zone when she herself was holding on to certain things. It was a bit of a conundrum. She supposed it was easier to encourage others than to take a hard look inward.

Give yourself grace. Poppy's words buzzed in her ears.

She needed to do that more often. Part of moving beyond the assault was allowing herself room to have setbacks and to truly stop the blame game.

"It wasn't my fault." She said the words out loud. Then she shouted them into the wind, over and over again until her voice sounded hoarse. When she heard the sound of tires crunching over the snow, Destiny realized that her last client of the day had arrived.

"I'm not to blame," she said in a firm tone before turning back toward the driveway and heading in the direction of her client.

Luke woke up bright and early the next morning to the sight of Java lying next to his bed on a cozy rug. He chuckled, fully entertained by the sight of the husky curled up into a ball. My, how quickly things had shifted. Java had him completely wrapped around her paw. She hadn't given him a single problem and he'd been able to work on some commands with the pup.

When it was time for bed, he'd put Java in the kitchen at first…until he'd had a change of heart and moved her into his bedroom. And it was a good thing he had. In the middle of the night he'd experienced an episode of night terrors, which had him reliving the deadly explosion. Thankfully these violent episodes had been rare as of late. Java had been right there at his side to soothe him. It was almost as if she'd known it was about to happen. That was how intuitive the sweet husky seemed to be.

Luke got out of bed and threw on a pair of sweatpants, a long-sleeved shirt and a warm parka before heading outside with Java. The weather had taken a bit of a turn, and he could feel the shift to colder temperatures taking hold.

Java began running around on his property as soon as she finished her business. The pup looked so happy as she darted back and forth, releasing pent-up energy. He didn't blame her one bit. This was true freedom and he yearned to feel this way again. He wanted to live his life without limitations.

When they headed back inside, Luke fixed Java her breakfast in a small mixing bowl from his cupboard. She hungrily wolfed it down, scraping the bowl clean. Luke could get used to this, despite all of his initial reservations. Java was great company and it was nice to not feel so alone. He hadn't realized until recently how lonely his existence had become. When he was in the service he'd never been without a team around him. Lots of chatter and camaraderie. He wasn't used to so much silence, and he was pretty sure that he didn't like it.

Once he'd eaten his own breakfast and taken a shower, Luke hung out at home for a while, doing online research and checking emails. His body froze as soon as a name came across his screen. Anita Martinez. Rico's mother. He slammed his computer shut and then pushed it away from him. Why was she reaching out to him? He hadn't seen or spoken to her since the memorial service nine months ago. He began to breathe heavily, his heart thundering in his chest. Java, sensing his distress, quickly came to sit beside him. She nudged his hand with her nose and comforted him.

"It's okay, girl. I'm okay," he said, trying to reassure her. The truth was, having Java around was calming. If she hadn't been here, Luke knew he would be spiraling. She was proving to be an amazing companion.

Did Anita want to confront him? Get firsthand details about the explosion? He stood up abruptly as a wave of dizziness swept over him. Java, sensing something was wrong, nuzzled his hand with her nose again. The dog's presence lifted him up.

He couldn't go down this road of communicating with the love of Rico's life. All it would do was drag him under to a dark place. Now that he was finally making progress, he couldn't afford any distractions.

He'd regained some equilibrium by the time they needed to head to Destiny's place. Java jumped up into the truck beside him without any prodding, which he knew was another sign of her intelligence. Throughout the ride she stayed close beside him, no doubt sensing his turbulent thoughts.

Having Java as a companion in the passenger seat had been a game changer.

The husky's presence had made a world of difference while driving his Range Rover. When he tensed up, she situated herself against his side, providing a type of comfort he couldn't put into words. Java was intuitive, sensing his distress as soon as it surfaced. Once he'd made it to the K9 farm and put his truck in Park, Java had nuzzled his hand with her nose as if to let him know he'd done a good job. Luke tousled her head as praise. It was amazing how easy it was to love her. They were really two peas in a pod.

As soon as he opened the door, Java jumped down and sat beside the vehicle, waiting for Luke's command. "Come on, girl. Let's go find Destiny."

The barn door was wide-open, the space practically overflowing with pups. A few ran over to greet Java. When he walked inside, Destiny was there with Isaac. They were both bent over at the waist with a Labrador retriever between them on a small table.

"Hey, Luke," Destiny said. "We're just patching up

one of the pups. This is Cosmo. He got into something he shouldn't have and deeply regrets it." Destiny looked down at the dog with an affectionate expression that left no doubt as to the way she felt about him. He wondered what it would be like to be the human object of her affection.

"Hi, Luke," Isaac said, keeping his attention focused on the dog. "What's up?"

"Hey there, Isaac. I can wait outside if you like," Luke offered. "Don't want to be a distraction."

"It's fine," Destiny said, standing up straight. "I think we're done here. Cosmo is much better now than when we started."

Luke could see that Cosmo had a medium-sized bandage on his leg. Isaac helped the Lab down to the ground and began walking with him outside. "I'll keep an eye on him," Isaac called out. Cosmo had a slight limp but he seemed to be walking pretty well overall. Life was certainly never dull around the K9 farm.

Luke, with Java at his side, walked toward her as she closed up a small first aid kit. With a knit cap on her head and a bright blue parka, she was definitely embracing the colder weather.

"I see you've got a lot of different skills," Luke said. "You're a regular Doctor Doolittle."

Destiny rolled her eyes as Luke chuckled. "Ha Ha. You're so funny."

"I try my best," he said with a slight nod of his head. It was nice to feel a bit lighter in spirit these days. Feeling so much heaviness on his shoulders had been exhausting.

"When you train as many service dogs as I do, it's imperative that you know how to handle all kinds of situations." A smile twitched at her lips. "I've become the dog whisperer."

"I won't argue with that," he said. He was impressed by her ability to cover all areas of care and training for her canines. It was obvious that she provided a good life for them until they were all sent to their forever homes.

The way she said it left no doubt that the dog whisperer title gave her great pleasure. Destiny appeared to be content with her life, which he envied. All he wanted in his own life was peace and a renewed sense of purpose. If he could achieve those things, he would be supremely grateful.

"So how did things go with Java?" she asked. "I was thinking about the two of you last night."

"Really well," he said, grinning. "She was perfect. Anytime I faltered she was right there beside me. Java was incredible when I had a bad nightmare. I really liked having her around."

"That's wonderful. I'm guessing she loved spending more one-on-one time with you," Destiny said, reaching out and gripping his arm. As soon as she touched him, he felt as if he'd been zapped by an electric shock.

She felt it too. He could tell by her self-conscious expression and the way she ducked her head to avoid eye contact. It was a heady feeling, knowing she wasn't immune to him. He'd spent a lot of time thinking about his growing attraction to her and wondering how much longer he could pretend it didn't matter. In a perfect world he could give voice to his feelings and put himself out there. But it was far from simple. He was still harboring a secret that he couldn't tell to a single soul, least of all Destiny.

He clenched his fists at his side. She would never look at him the same way if she discovered he was the opposite of a hero. The very thought of Destiny finding out caused his body to tense up. How many times had she referenced his heroism as a SEAL? More times than he could count.

Java, sensing his anxiety, didn't hesitate to try and comfort him. She was licking his hand and sticking close to his side.

"Hey. Earth to Luke. Are you listening?" She was staring at him as if he was an alien from another planet.

"Yeah, sure. Sorry. I just zoned out for a moment." Little did she know his thoughts had been consumed by her.

"I was saying that the Alaskan Moon festival would be a great event to test the waters with Java." She looked at him expectantly.

He frowned. "In that crowded setting?" Just the thought of doing a training exercise at the festival caused his heart to ricochet inside his chest. He was still avoiding going into town at this point, which meant he hadn't been exposed to the Serenity Peak community. He couldn't just show up at the festival and try to blend in. Small towns didn't work like that.

Destiny nodded. "As you know, it does get a bit congested."

"I'm not sure that I'm ready to be front and center like that," he admitted. He hated being this tentative, but it was best to be honest. How could he commit to her plan while harboring serious concerns about the event? If he agreed to participate, would it be caving under the pressure? The worst scenario would be letting Destiny down—in front of everyone. After all she'd done for him, it was a painful thought.

"You're more than ready, skillwise. You and Java are gelling beautifully. But only you know if it's something you can handle emotionally." She ran a hand through her wavy hair. "I would never presume to make that judgment call for you. All I can tell you is that I believe in you."

Although it was nice to hear positive affirmations from Destiny, uncertainty nagged at him. For the past year he'd been struggling with anxiety, flashbacks, massive guilt and doubt. Pushing past those issues in order to accomplish this task would be difficult. Yet, a part of him wanted to see if it was possible. A year ago, something like this would have been a piece of cake for him. He felt humbled at how far he'd fallen.

"My concern is the setting. Is that really something I need to focus on at the moment?" he asked, not wanting to limit his progress.

"Well, to be honest, that's going to be your reality pretty soon, Luke. Being in places with loads of people is hard to avoid at times. You said that you wanted to get back into the world, and that's a part of it." She was speaking gently to him and he sensed that Destiny didn't want to push too hard.

All of a sudden his confidence plummeted. So far everything had been going really well with his service training, but introducing this new dynamic might throw it all into chaos. It could literally be six steps forward, eight steps back.

The festival had been a staple of their childhood, celebrating the arrival of autumn in a big way. Everyone in Serenity Peak attended, as well as tourists and Alaskans from neighboring towns. It was a huge town event with lots of bells and whistles. He hadn't attended in years due to being deployed, but anytime he'd been able to go to the festival, he'd always had an amazing time. For Luke, the event was nostalgic.

Destiny continued. "I think getting you out to actual events in the community is the best way to hone your developing skills. And it will be practical for your future."

Luke bit the inside of his cheek. He knew it would be tricky for him to deal with crowds of people and their questions. He hadn't exactly announced his presence in town. Just the thought of explaining his circumstances seemed excruciating. How could he make Destiny understand? It was what he'd been avoiding ever since his return.

But he also knew no guts, no glory. Titus Brandt, his commander, had said it to his team almost every single day. Life was hard, with no promises of a straightforward path. Sometimes a person just had to clamp down and focus on the challenges that awaited them. SEAL service had drummed that into his head.

The Navy Seal motto came to mind. *The only easy day was yesterday.*

Destiny took a step toward him, so close that he could smell the scent of vanilla hovering around her. All he could focus on was her. His gut tightened at her close proximity. Luke couldn't remember the last time he'd been so attracted to a woman. The fact that he'd always thought of Destiny as Charlie's little sister was mind-blowing. She was so much more than that and she always had been. As a kid, she had been plucky and full of grit. As a woman, she was full of strength and integrity.

"I promise to be there with you. You're not in this alone. I can guarantee you that."

He sensed that she was a woman who kept her promises. And they would be in this together, which was comforting.

"I'll give it a go," he said after a few moments, a ragged sigh slipping past his lips. This was a big deal to him. And hopefully, it would be an incredible milestone for his service dog training.

Her face lit up. "That's great. It'll be an awesome experience." She smiled up at him. "At this rate you might even graduate from the program ahead of time."

He leaned in toward her, feeling playful as his tension dissipated. "Am I getting high marks from the teacher?"

Destiny shook her head. Her cheeks looked slightly flushed. "So far, you're getting all A's," she quipped. "But if we don't get this lesson started soon, I might have to give you an incomplete."

Luke let out a hearty chuckle. He loved the relaxed moments between them, when it wasn't about the service dog training and they were just responding to one another in a natural way. Just the sound of her tinkling laughter caused a pang in the region of his heart. It took him all the way back to their childhood of building forts in the woods and catching salamanders in the brook. He loved that they were getting closer with every day that passed and rebuilding their old bond.

Maybe, just maybe, he could summon the courage to tell her about the secret he'd been harboring without it all blowing up in his face.

Chapter Seven

"You made plans to meet up with Thad tomorrow?" Destiny tried to keep the surprise from ringing out in her voice. She didn't want Luke to second-guess his plans based on her response. He was making amazing strides with Java, and he was also opening himself up to new possibilities. Not too long ago he'd run away from an encounter with his former teacher, and now he had taken steps to repair that situation.

The pride she felt in him threatened to burst from her chest. The feeling was both exhilarating and terrifying. Luke was a client and a childhood friend. Should she really be feeling so invested in all of his accomplishments?

Luke nodded. "I reached out to him a few days ago after Java stayed over at my place." He quirked his mouth. "I think that experience gave me the courage to push myself a little bit further." He knit his brows together. "Thoughts?"

"I think it's absolutely wonderful," she said. "I'm guessing he was thrilled to hear from you." The last time Thad dropped by, he'd told her all about his pride in his favorite former student.

"He was pretty stoked from what I could tell." Luke looked pretty happy himself.

"Thad is a bit like Buzz. He lost his wife a few years ago, but he's very social and loves to be out and about in town."

He shifted from one foot to the other. "There's one other thing. I was wondering if I can keep Java tonight. I have a lot of butterflies about this meeting with Thad since it'll be my first solo trip into town. Not to mention I'm dreading having to explain my situation to him."

"That's a great idea, Luke. I don't see a problem with Java staying with you, especially since you'll be out in the field with her, practicing things you've been working on."

"I suppose it'll be a field trip of sorts," Luke said. "I used to love those back when we were in school."

Luke had been an active and outgoing kid, always excited about exploration and pushing past boundaries. It was nice to see a little bit of that coming back to life.

"And that's a good thing. You'll be able to really test your skills." Her voice oozed with excitement. She was passionate about her work, and in moments like this one, she felt like jumping up and down with joy.

"Remember, it's important to command Java to lie down by herself and stay put. Don't lavish her with attention or do anything to distract her from doing the job at hand. Since she's in the training stage with you, don't allow folks to pet her. That's always challenging because people love huskies and know they're super friendly. Getting past that awkwardness is important."

"Okay. Got it. And she should be wearing a red vest as well, right?"

"Very good question. The vest basically lets everyone know that she's a service dog. Most establishments in town allow all service dogs entry, so that shouldn't be a problem if you want to eat somewhere or shop."

"I'm not sure that I'll be that adventurous, but it's good to know," Luke said.

All of sudden Isaac appeared, out of breath and visibly agitated. "Boss, we have a problem," he said. "One of the pups escaped the yard. She was running so fast I couldn't catch her, and I didn't want to leave the other dogs."

"Oh no. Which pup was it?" she asked, even though she had a good idea that it was Lemon, a feisty terrier.

"It was Lemon," Isaac confirmed. "I figured that I needed reinforcements up here. Maybe you could take your truck and search while I watch the rest of the pups."

"Smart thinking," Destiny said, looking over at Luke. "I'm sorry. I've got to run before something happens to Lemon. She's pretty young and fast on her paws."

"Don't apologize. I was about to suggest that I come along with you. Two pairs of eyes are better than one."

Destiny let out the breath she'd been holding. The situation was stressful. Luke's offer was greatly appreciated. "That would be great. I can drive if you're willing to jump out if we come across Lemon. She's a fast one though."

"Sounds like a plan," Luke said. "I'm glad that I ate my Wheaties this morning."

Although Destiny knew he was teasing, her heart was racing at the possibility of the small pup being in a dangerous situation. What if she was hit by a car or veered off into the woods? So many things could go wrong.

They raced over to Destiny's truck and jumped inside, Luke riding shotgun. Once she revved the engine, Destiny steered the vehicle out of the driveway and toward the main road. All the while she sent up prayers that this was the way Lemon had traveled.

She bit her lip. "There's so much snow on the ground now. It's going to make it difficult to spot her white fur."

"Don't worry, Destiny. We've got this. Lemon is coming home to you." His voice sounded steady and true. He spoke with such authority that it gave her hope that she would be reunited with her dog.

"I really hope so," she said before uttering a silent prayer that it would come to pass. Each of her pups was special to her with unique personalities and special skills. Lemon hadn't even begun her service training yet. She had so much to learn and share with the world. It was painful to imagine something happening to her.

His left arm rested solidly against her right one and the contact was comforting. She wasn't alone in this. Luke was proving to be a strong source of support.

As she drove along at a slow pace, they both kept their eyes peeled to their surroundings. If they ventured off this road, Destiny thought the chances of finding Lemon would be diminished. Her heart sank at the possibility of not finding the sweet pup.

All of a sudden, Luke cried out, "Stop! Stop the truck!" Destiny hit the brakes and scanned in the direction he was pointing toward. "There she is," he said urgently.

She looked in the distance, but she didn't see anything.

"Right there by the copse of trees," he said. "That splash of color."

Just then Destiny saw a little blob of white accented by her bright yellow collar. "Oh my gosh. You're right. There she is."

Luke wrenched open the door and took off like a shot without another word. He cut across the field at top speed,

his rugged build propelling him toward Lemon. Clea
he was still in incredible shape, displaying an athleticis.
that most would envy.

She rolled down her window and could hear Luke calling Lemon's name, but like the rascal she was, the terrier
didn't stop. Luke's speed increased, and she watched as he
reached down and scooped Lemon up as if he was a foot-
ball player grabbing the ball. Destiny flung open the door
and vaulted to the ground. She met Luke halfway, yelling
and screaming with excitement.

He held Lemon out to her and she cradled the pup in her
arms. "You've been such a naughty girl, but I'm so happy
to see your little face, safe and sound," she crooned as she
nuzzled her nose in Lemon's fur. The pup lifted her head
up and regarded Destiny with innocent eyes. Both Luke
and Destiny cracked up.

"She's a terror," Luke said, ruffling her fur. "She gave
me quite a workout."

"She sure is," Destiny agreed, "but I'm so thankful she's
back." She touched Luke's arm. 'I'm super grateful to you,
Luke."

"I'm glad that I could be here to help out," he said. "You're
always the one helping me, so turnabout is fair play."

A feeling of contentment settled over her as they drove
back to the property with Lemon sitting beside them. For
so long Destiny had refused to lean on anyone, not even her
family. She'd convinced herself that in order to prove she
was strong and resilient, she had to go it alone. But today
she'd leaned on Luke, and he hadn't disappointed her. It
felt nice to partner up with him and solve a crisis together.

And it made her wonder. What would it feel like to have
him as a permanent part of her world?

* * *

Making his way into town wasn't as traumatic as he'd imagined. In the past he had given up every single time and turned his truck around to head back home. Today, on his way to meet up with Thad, felt different. It wasn't only Java's presence that was bolstering him, though that helped. This morning he had placed a red vest on Java so she would easily be recognized as a service animal. Plus, Luke had a bit more confidence now due to the fact that he'd assisted Destiny in finding her runaway pup, Lemon. It had been a long time since he'd used his skills to help others. Being of use in that manner had made him feel ten feet tall. Destiny's gratitude had been effusive. He also had his service training to ground him.

So as he drove, he kept reminding himself that if things became difficult he could pull over to collect himself. Java seemed to sense that this was a big deal, because she was on alert and paying attention to all of his movements and emotions.

Clearly, working with Java had made all the difference in the world. When she sensed his anxiety, Java nuzzled her nose against him or snuggled up beside him. She was an intuitive dog and it was a no-brainer that she'd become a service dog. She had all the qualities of the perfect therapy dog.

"You were born to do this, weren't you?" he asked Java after parking on Main Street. He leaned over so that his face was next to the Husky's, and she responded by licking his face. Luke laughed as Java lavished him with affection. He couldn't even pretend not to be tickled. His fondness for Java was off the charts. She had quickly nestled her way into his heart.

When he walked into the Humbled coffee shop, Luke noticed a sign on the door welcoming service dogs into the establishment. This was all new to him. He felt silly admitting it, but he'd never paid too much attention to therapy dogs.

He made his way to a table in the back as soon as he spotted Mr. Josephs sitting with his own service dog. The older man was dressed casually in a pair of worn jeans and a cardigan sweater.

"Good morning, young man," he said in a booming voice when Luke reached the table.

"Morning, Mr. Josephs," he said, warmly greeting him as he took a seat across from him.

"Please call me Thad. You're no longer my student. We're on equal footing now."

"Okay. Thad it is," Luke agreed. "This is Java," he said, appreciating the way the pup sat down next to him without being distracted by the other dog or the patrons.

The café was a little more crowded than he'd envisioned. The odds of seeing someone he'd grown up with were fairly high. He'd practiced a few responses at home in his bathroom mirror. His main objective was not to get flustered or zone out. As his therapist had once told him, people were well-meaning and simply expressing their curiosity. He would try to remember that.

"Nice to meet you, Java. This is Lottie," Thad said, looking down at the Labrador retriever, who was also calmly resting at his feet. "She helps me with my blood sugar. Alerts me anytime my numbers go too high or too low. It's pretty uncanny."

"It's a whole new world for me," Luke acknowledged. "I'm learning a lot about service dogs and the variety of people who require them in their lives."

The waitress popped by and took their order—a Frappuccino and a chocolate croissant for Luke and an espresso and a slice of banana bread for Thad.

"Thanks for meeting me," Luke said, drumming his fingers on the table. He had no idea how to get the ball rolling.

"I was hoping to hear from you," Thad said. "You've been in my thoughts a lot over the years. I imagine you were flying high as a SEAL."

Luke grimaced. "Until about a year ago, I was. I'm no longer deployed. I'm sorry about being so abrupt with you at the K9 farm. I'd like to explain." Although he was a bit nervous, he knew that he owed his old friend an explanation.

He nodded. "By the way, Destiny was very discreet. She didn't divulge anything to me." Thad sent Luke a knowing look. "You've got a great friend in that girl."

Friend? Truth be told, he was feeling a little more than friendship toward her. Ignoring the little flutter in his stomach when he was around her wasn't working. She always seemed to be in his thoughts.

"She's a good woman," Luke acknowledged. "I'm learning a lot through her program."

"Were you wounded, son?" Thad's gaze narrowed as he looked at him. "If you're not comfortable discussing this with me, we can change the subject. No worries."

Luke clenched his jaw and splayed his hands out on the table. It still wasn't easy to talk about the explosion, but he knew discussing it was important to his recovery.

He bowed his head for a moment, trying to find the words. "My SEAL team and I were hit by an IED in Cameroon. We were riding in a Humvee when it happened without warning," Luke explained. "It was a horrific blast."

Thad let out a shocked sound. "Oh, how horrible. I'm so sorry."

"It was absolutely catastrophic. Two of my SEAL buddies succumbed to their injuries." He let out a ragged breath. "I wasn't hurt physically. All of my wounds are psychological ones," he admitted. He had to force the words out of his mouth, since it still wasn't easy admitting that he had PTSD. In his mind he'd always believed that being a SEAL meant he was mentally strong. These days he wasn't so sure.

"Surviving a blast that killed your friends is devastating." Thad ran a shaky hand across his jaw. "I can't imagine what you endured. What you witnessed."

Luke wouldn't wish the experience on his worst enemy. The attack had upended his entire world. He continued to suffer from the aftereffects and he had no idea when this nightmare would end.

"Honestly, I haven't been the same since. That's why I'm working with Java. And Destiny." He cleared his throat. "I suffer from anxiety and panic attacks."

Thad nodded, looking thoughtful. "I'm not surprised after all you've been through. Getting help shows strength. It's the best path toward getting your life back."

"I appreciate you saying so." His former teacher had always been empathetic and kind, as well as a wonderful role model. Thad had always encouraged Luke to shoot for the stars. And to the best of his ability, he had.

"In my humble opinion, Destiny is the best person to train you. She's walked your walk. She had the sweetest little service dog until she passed away." Thad shook his head. "They were an inspirational duo."

Luke was tongue-tied. He didn't have a single clue as

to how to respond to this nugget of information. It was odd that Destiny had never mentioned her own experience with a service dog. Although he was extremely curious, he couldn't pry by asking why she'd needed a service animal. And he wasn't going to ask Destiny either. If she wanted him to know, she would tell him on her own terms.

"So what else are you doing to keep busy? I imagine it hasn't been easy no longer being a SEAL."

"Believe it or not, I've been painting and drawing. I've tapped into my creative side, and it centers me," Luke told him. It was invigorating talking about his passion for painting, something only a few people knew about. Although he did it for fun and relaxation, Rosie couldn't stop raving about how talented he was, which was flattering and a bit hard to believe.

Thad tapped his chin. "I'm not surprised at all. I seem to remember you painting back in high school."

"You're right. I sure did," he said, blown away by the recollection.

Luke wasn't sure why he'd blocked that out. So much of his free time had been spent in the art studio at school. Like now, it had served as a creative outlet. Somehow over the years, his focus had shifted to other pursuits. He'd forgotten how much he loved immersing himself in sketching and painting.

By the time they had wrapped up their coffee meetup, they'd made plans to get together again in a few weeks. Not long ago the idea of driving into town would have seemed impossible. He was proud of himself for pushing past a barrier and making progress. These days, that was what it was all about.

After saying his goodbyes to Thad, Luke headed toward

the counter to pick up a cinnamon bun for Rosie. His sister had a serious sweet tooth that she regularly indulged in. She'd always been so supportive of him, so much so that he liked to do little gestures to show her that she was appreciated. This would do the trick.

The bell behind him jingled, announcing a customer's arrival. He slightly turned his head, recognizing the woman by the tilt of her head and the coppery highlights in her brown hair.

"Destiny!" he said, turning around to face her. As usual, the sight of her made adrenaline rush through his body.

He tried to silence the voice inside of him that wanted to shout out with joy at the sight of her. *Play it cool*, he reminded himself. They were in the friend zone. And if he knew what was good for him, he would keep things firmly planted there.

"Luke! Fancy running into you here." Destiny looked down at the ground where Java was patiently seated. It was nice to see that Luke was putting into practice the tips she'd given him about using commands with Java to avoid distractions. "Hey, Java! Aren't you a sight for sore eyes." It was amazing how quickly she missed one of her pups if they were away from home. They always eventually left her in order to live with their handlers in their forever homes, but each dog nuzzled their way into her heart well before their departure.

"I just had coffee with Thad."

She didn't think she'd ever seen Luke grin so wide. At least not since they were kids. Joy looked good on him.

"I'm so glad the two of you met up." Destiny knew Luke had a long road to full recovery, but she could see more flashes of the old Luke. He was lighter somehow and show-ing more confidence. Training with Java was helping him.

"I can't tell you how great it was to reconnect with him. It was cool socializing as adults, not as teacher and student."

"Well you sure chose a great place. I'm here to pick up some baked goods for Buzz and to browse the shelves. He's hosting some of his buddies for book club."

"That's brilliant. Buzz seems to be living his best life."

Destiny loved Luke's sentiment. Why shouldn't her grandfather have joyful moments? At his age, and after losing Junie, he needed to seize the moments and live it up. *Carpe diem*.

"Who's holding down the fort for you back at the farm?" Luke asked.

"Isaac is keeping an eye on the dogs until I get back. I'm only here due to a cancellation. My client is sick with a stomach bug. I figured I'd stop by one of my favorite places since I have a block of free time."

"It's a great shop. Humbled is new to me, but I love the concept," Luke raved. He waved his arm around him. "A café on one side, bookstore on the other. It doesn't get bet-ter than that."

She felt a grin tugging at her lips. This place was a total dream. In a perfect world, she could browse the shelves for-ever. "The best of both worlds. Do you remember Molly Truitt? She totally reinvented this place."

"This is her place? That's great."

They had all been in school together. Years ago her grandfather had owned the coffee shop, but it had been nothing like this new and improved version. Molly had given it a glow up and added space to create a haven for booklovers. Judging by how packed the place always seemed to be, it was a success.

"I like to browse the bookshop to find classic copies of Nancy Drew mysteries," Destiny told him. "Every now and then I spot one for my collection. It totally makes my day. That's what I'm up to now."

"Mind if Java and I tag along?" Luke asked. "I need a new book to read."

"Of course not," Destiny said cheerfully. "I appreciate the company."

The bookstore was a modest-sized space stacked with rows and rows of books in brightly colored shelves. Pinks. Blues. Greens. The aesthetic was upbeat and beautiful. It was definitely one of her designated happy places. She had always been a huge reader and this bookstore gave her the warm and fuzzies.

Luke flashed her a knowing look. "I remember you always had your nose stuck in a Nancy Drew book. Nice to know some things never change."

Destiny let out a cry of surprise. "I can't believe you remember that. I'm actually trying to recreate my childhood collection." She made a face. "My copies were ruined when my parent's basement flooded."

"What a shame. I know they must've meant a lot to you." His expression was sympathetic. "Childhood keepsakes."

"It's okay," she reassured him. "My new collection is shaping up quite nicely. I've been searching the shop for number one for a while now." She let out a little sigh.

"*Secret of the Old Clock*, right?"

"Hey. How did you know that?" she asked. "Only die-hard fans have that information."

"You weren't the only one who enjoyed the titian haired sleuth." He chuckled.

She stopped in the middle of an aisle and looked at him, open-mouthed. "Really? I only remember you reading Sherlock Holmes."

He turned away and began perusing the shelves. "That too. I had a thing for mysteries. I always loved being transported away from my everyday life in Serenity Peak."

"Is that why you became a SEAL?" Destiny had been curious as to how Luke's Navy SEAL journey had begun. What had inspired him to reach those heights?

"In part. I always dreamed of traveling all over the world and helping people."

"Well, you sure achieved that goal, didn't you?"

She watched as he plucked a book from the shelf. "I did," he said with a nod. "That's something no one can ever take away from me."

His comment made her think about all that he'd lost. Being a Navy SEAL had given him a sense of self. A purpose that involved helping others. He must be asking himself who he was without his military service. Without all the accolades and the missions.

"No, they can't, Luke. You definitely earned that title." And many more, she wanted to add. He was a bona fide hero. Not many people could claim that title.

It was nice spending time with Luke outside of service training. And it was reassuring to see him vibing so well with Java in a setting that wasn't the K9 farm. All of her suspicions about Luke and Java making a great team were correct. To look at the two of them, one might think that they'd been together for years rather than weeks.

Destiny purchased a few books while Luke picked up a

spy thriller and a journal for himself. It was nice to see that he was doing things to improve his outlook. She picked up Buzz's treats while Luke bought a cinnamon roll.

Luke held the door open for her as they headed outside. They had barely stepped out of the shop when a loud series of bangs rang out, interrupting the tranquility of Main Street. She felt strong arms around her as he pulled her against the building. He was shielding her with his body, although she had no idea what was going on. Everything was happening so fast. All she could focus on was Luke's face—the dazed expression, the widened eyes, the fear.

She looked around and realized that the loud noises had come from a service truck a few feet away. "Sorry about that," a man standing beside the truck called out to them. "This keeps happening. Gotta put it back in the shop." He threw his hands up in frustration.

Destiny turned back to Luke, who was breathing heavily. She wasn't sure if he'd even heard the driver's explanation.

"It's just a car backfiring. We're fine," she said in a soothing voice.

He didn't respond but simply looked straight through her as if she wasn't there. His eyes were completely vacant. Luke was in a world of his own at the moment.

"What's happening, Luke? Talk to me!" She was tugging at his arm now, frantic to get him to speak or at least acknowledge her presence.

He slumped against the wall. Luke raised his hand to his chest. "I—I can't breathe. My heart is about to escape out of my chest." Java was right next to him, providing comfort. She had quickly recognized Luke's distress and was doing her best to help him. She was pressing her nose against him and licking his hand.

"I think you're having a panic attack," she said. Destiny had experienced a few of her own in the past and she knew how terrifying they could be. Sometimes it seemed as if one was dying or having a heart attack.

"I—I need to go home," he muttered, walking away. He wasn't steady on his feet and he stumbled. "Take Java for me."

"You shouldn't drive right now, Luke. Please." Destiny clutched his arm while holding Java's leash in her free hand.

"I—I just need to get out here. And be by myself." His breathing was choppy and beads of sweat pooled on his forehead. Her heart went out to him. He was in acute distress.

"Let me walk you toward your truck. Is that all right?" She didn't know why she was asking him, because she wasn't going to take no for an answer. He wasn't in great shape at the moment and she had no intention of leaving him alone. Luke must've sensed her determination, since he quietly agreed with a slight nod. A few minutes later they were standing beside his Range Rover.

She got in the vehicle and sat in the passenger seat with Java between them. Luke sat back in the driver's seat with his eyes closed. He folded his arms across his chest until Java settled in his lap and nuzzled her nose against him. Luke rubbed her back and murmured to her. He pressed his face against Java's fur and exhaled deeply. In return, Java licked Luke's cheek. He seemed a bit more relaxed now, with his breathing less choppy.

"I'm so sorry, Luke. I know that must have been really terrifying for you."

His body shuddered. "I had a flashback to the explosion.

It all felt so real. The sounds. The loud noises. It seemed like an elephant was standing on my chest."

"I know what a panic attack feels like. I've had quite a few myself," she admitted. It was one of the worst feelings in the world, to be gasping for breath and believing you were at death's door.

"You're not just saying that to make me feel better, are you?" he asked. The look in his eyes was heartbreaking— a mix of dread and uncertainty.

"No, I'm not. I promise." Now wasn't the time to tell him about her past, but she wanted him to know that he wasn't alone in feeling this way.

"Why is this so hard for me?" he asked, his voice laced with pain. "I used to think my SEAL status made me tough, but I was wrong." He let out an agonized sound.

"Hey, you've got to give yourself a break. You went through a traumatic event. Those leave scars, ones that take time to heal."

She reached out and placed her palm on his chest right above his heart. "Just take deep breaths so your heart rate settles down." He began breathing in and out slowly, over and over again. It seemed to be working. His body began to relax and his breathing became steadier.

Destiny turned on the radio, allowing the soft rhythms of an easy listening station to wash over them. After a few moments he began to hum along with the song. Much to her relief, he was coming back around. The panic attack was fading away.

"I think the worst is over," Destiny said. "You're going to be all right."

"Can you sit with me a bit longer? Would that be okay?" he asked in a low tone. Luke's vulnerability threatened to crack her heart wide-open. She knew a tough Navy SEAL like him wasn't used to leaning on others, but that was his old life, she realized. This was now. And he needed her.

"Of course I can," she said, leaning toward Luke. Java scooted over to make room for her. On pure instinct she wrapped her arms around Luke and tightly held on to him. Although her gesture was one of comfort, Destiny couldn't ignore his rugged appeal or the heady scent of his woodsy aftershave.

"Lord," she said aloud, "Please deliver Luke from this overwhelming sense of panic and dread. Bring peace to his heart so that he may heal."

"Amen," Luke said. By the time she let go, Luke was no longer trembling. When he looked at her, his eyes radiated gratitude.

"I appreciate you being here, Destiny," Luke said, his voice sounding back to normal. "More than you'll ever know."

"There's no place I'd rather be," she murmured. And she meant it. Luke was becoming more important to her with every passing day. Although he was the one signed up for training, Luke was teaching her so much about herself. And moving past her own trauma. Although she was further along in the healing process than he was, sometimes it felt as if she was looking in a mirror. She had walked his road and knew the challenges as well as the pitfalls.

And in this tender moment between them, she realized that being in such close proximity to Luke wasn't scary or overwhelming. She had held him. Comforted him. Prayed for him. They had been alone in a small space. At no time had she flinched or frozen up. She had simply leaned into the moment. Into Luke. She trusted this man.

And now, a huge weight had been lifted off her shoulders, one she'd been carrying around for years. She may have been bent by the assault, but she wasn't broken.

Chapter Eight

For the past few days all Luke could think about was the incident outside Humbled with Destiny. He was wrestling with so many emotions. Luke couldn't help but feel an overwhelming sense of embarrassment. He was disgusted with himself. Not being able to control the flashbacks and the panic attacks made him feel weak. After so many years of being known for his strength, it was a bitter pill to swallow. Being a SEAL meant being tough in all areas, so perhaps it was fitting that he was now retired.

Due to feeling overwhelmed, he had canceled his next training session with Java and Destiny. He'd left a message on Destiny's answering machine, making up an excuse about being sick. He couldn't imagine that she would buy his story, but at the moment he was simply trying to push down all of the things that had come bubbling to the surface in the past few days. Hopefully she understood and wouldn't hold it against him.

Now he was at his parents' house for Sunday dinner, washing the dishes with Rosie after the meal. Jeff and Rebecca Adams were loving, yet they struggled to connect with their children. Neither one seemed to understand his PTSD and why he'd been struggling. They believed that mental health was simply mind over matter. Through a veil of tears his mother had said, "I just want the old Luke back. The one who made us so proud." Ouch. He had bitten his tongue rather than let her know that he too wanted his old life back and simply wishing it didn't make it come true. He had learned a long time ago that neither of his parents were capable of empathy unless it was for each other. Luke loved them dearly, but he couldn't count on them for support during this time of healing.

Needing a shoulder to lean on, Luke had told his sister all about the devastating flashback and the aftermath as they hung out in the kitchen doing chores.

"Destiny was really amazing, walking me to my truck and basically holding my hand until my body and mind settled down," he told his sister. His respect and admiration for Destiny had grown exponentially. She was an incredible woman with a caring heart.

"Sounds deep. Did you kiss her?" Rosie asked. Her eyes were sparkling with interest, and he knew his sister was intrigued by his connection to Destiny.

"No, I didn't, Rosie," he said, not in the slightest bit shocked that she'd asked. This was quintessential Rosie— never afraid to speak her mind with a penchant for being blunt. He shook his head. "What part of a panic attack don't you understand? It wasn't exact the right time or place."

Rosie cocked her head to the side. "But you want to, right? I can tell."

He skirted the question by saying, "I don't know if that's what she wants. It's complicated."

"It doesn't sound that complicated. Clearly there's something between the two of you. Right? You're not the sort of person to imagine that type of connection." She reached out and squeezed his cheek playfully. "And who wouldn't fall for you? Tall, dark and handsome. You were definitely at the front of the line when the good Lord handed out good looks."

Laughter bubbled up inside of him. Rosie said the funniest things. "You have to say nice things about me. I'm your baby brother," Luke said. He loved this connection he and Rosie shared. His admiration for his sibling had increased tenfold after seeing her deal with an MS diagnosis with such courage and grace. And now her marriage was ending. No matter what lemons life dealt her, Rosie always held her head up high and carried on with living. He definitely could learn a lot from the way she lived her life.

"You're a catch, Luke. And don't you forget it," she said, wagging her finger at him.

"Aww, shucks. You're going to give me a swelled head." He flicked some dish soap in her direction, starting a little kitchen war.

Thank the good Lord for big sisters. She was always lifting him up to the stratosphere with compliments and praise. She was a blessing.

Luke couldn't tell Rosie one of the main reasons he was uncertain about anything happening between him and Destiny. He was holding back on exploring his budding feelings out of fear. What would happen if he told Destiny his secret and she rejected him? The pain would be hard to bear. That was the reason he hadn't told a single soul—not even Rosie—that he blamed himself for the deaths of his SEAL buddies.

He knew his feelings for her were intensifying as time went by. She was way more to him than a childhood friend or a K9 trainer. He was afraid to even put it into words, because he knew that he wasn't in any position to be in a relationship. How could he be, with all of the baggage he was carrying around? And the secret that weighed him down? For so long now he'd asked God to pardon him, to relieve some of this pressure. So far those prayers hadn't been answered. Plus, there was the issue of what he sensed she wasn't telling him. Maybe Rosie could help him there.

He shrugged. "I get the feeling she's holding a part of herself back." He felt like a hypocrite saying so, since he himself was doing the same thing. But two things could be true at the same time.

"Why do you say that?" Rosie asked, frowning. "She's always been such a straightforward person."

He began stacking the dried dishes in the cabinet. "When Thad Josephs and I met up for coffee he mentioned that Destiny had her own service dog that had passed away. She's never once mentioned it."

"Everyone has things they keep under wraps." Rosie handed him some washed utensils. "Life taught me a long time ago that we all have battles we're fighting. Some, like yours, aren't visible to the eye. It's not exactly the type of thing you can ask her without seeming intrusive." Rosie rolled her eyes. "Trust me, I've been asked countless questions about my MS, and since I've been back in Serenity Peak, folks think nothing about asking me about the state of my marriage. And if I plan on having any kids."

"I'm sorry about that, Rosie," he said, wishing he could step in and solve all of his sister's problems. The truth was, he couldn't even fix his own.

Rosie's comments made Luke think. He wasn't trying to invade her privacy, but he wanted to know everything he possibly could about the adult version of his childhood pal.

Why hadn't she mentioned her own experience with

a service dog? When Luke had originally asked her why she'd ventured into service training, he'd had sensed that her answer hadn't been complete. Now he was certain that she'd deliberately left something out.

A personal angle. He shouldn't feel so curious about her service dog, but he couldn't deny that he was. Had she been involved in an accident? Or was it something else? Destiny had told him she knew what it was like to have a panic attack and that she'd had a few herself. *Stop prying,* he told himself. He was being ridiculous.

"So, fess up. Are you falling for her?" Rosie had a dishrag in one hand and a serving bowl in the other. She was gazing at him intensely.

The question had been one he'd been asking himself as of late. Falling for her would be as easy as skipping stones on Kachemak Bay, but what came after? That would be all kinds of complicated. Wasn't his life already riddled with complexities?

"I like her," he admitted. "But falling in love isn't in the game plan, even with someone as amazing as Destiny. I need to focus on getting my life back. Destiny is a wonderful woman, but life is all about timing. It isn't the right time for me to have such serious feelings for someone."

Rosie let out a harsh laugh. "Luke. I hate to break it to you, but falling in love isn't something you can plan or prevent. It just happens, like a bolt of lightning or a comet soaring through the sky." She lightly slapped him on the back. "And from the way you sound when you talk about her, I'm guessing you're well on your way."

While a part of his brain rejected the notion, another part knew that his older sister was rarely wrong about anything.

Now more than ever, Luke would just have to make sure they stayed friends and nothing more.

By the time Luke made his way back to her K9 farm, a week had gone by since the incident at Humbled. Even though Destiny had wanted to call Luke to check on him, she'd resisted the impulse. Attending the training sessions was vitally important to his overall success in the program. If he started skipping sessions, his bond with Java would be diminished. As it was, Destiny could tell that the sweet husky was on the lookout for Luke. She was practically in mourning for him.

She wasn't sure what to think about his absence. Was he really sick or was it directly related to the panic attack he'd suffered? As soon as she spotted his Range Rover pulling into the yard, a feeling of relief swept over her. Java wasn't the only one who had missed Luke in his absence. She couldn't deny her own feelings about his disappearing act. She had acutely missed him during his time away from her K9 farm.

She greeted him with a wave, keeping a professional distance between them. "Glad to see you're back." She had been waiting with Java outside in the hopes of seeing him pull up in her driveway.

"Glad to be back," he said, his expression shuttered. Sometimes she wished that she could gauge his mood and feelings, but as a SEAL, Destiny knew he had been trained to mask them.

"Java! Come!" Luke commanded. Without skipping a beat, Java ran to his side, wagging her tail with every step she took.

"She missed you," Destiny said. *And she wasn't the only*

one. The thought threw her off-kilter. She had no business missing a client! Especially one who was as good-looking as Luke. What was this sensation fluttering around in her stomach? She didn't know whether to laugh or cry about it.

He twisted his mouth. "It couldn't be helped. I just needed to decompress a little bit," he explained. "I wasn't feeling that well."

"That happens to all of us from time to time, but keeping the schedule is important. I would be remiss in my duties if I didn't remind you of that," she told him. She kept her voice crisp and professional.

"Point taken," Luke said. He took a step closer toward her. "I have something for you. Just a little thank-you for all you've done to help me train with Java. You've truly gone above and beyond. He held out a festively wrapped parcel.

"For me?" she asked, overwhelmed by the gesture. It was always special when a client thought of her in this way. It was never necessary, but always appreciated.

He winked at her. "Unless you don't want it of course," he said, sounding playful. He pulled the wrapped parcel away.

Destiny let out a cry of protest. "Hey, give it back. I'm dying to open it. I was always up at the crack of dawn on Christmas morning to open my gifts."

"I can totally picture that," he said. His smile was nice and easy, as if all the hard stuff was a distant memory. He seemed to be in a much better headspace today. Maybe the time away from training had given him some perspective.

Destiny began to unwrap the gift, being gentle at first until sheer excitement caused her to rip off the packaging. As soon as she saw the name Carolyn Keene she gasped.

Luke had managed to track down the Nancy Drew book she'd been looking for—*The Secret of the Old Clock*.

She immediately lifted it to her nose and inhaled the scent of an old book. "Oh, Luke. What an incredible gift." She pressed the book against her chest and let out a big sigh. "This really brings me back to my childhood. Thank you so very much. I can't wait to put it on my keeper shelf."

"It's just a small token of my gratitude," Luke said. "Something to make you smile. In case no one's told you, your smile is terrific."

The compliment went straight to her head, causing her cheeks to flush. She was normally so professional but now she felt almost giddy. Why did Luke always make her feel like that twelve-year-old girl who'd nurtured a huge crush on him?

She locked gazes with him. "You didn't have to, but I'm glad you did," she said. "It means a lot to me."

"I've been doing so much better overall. I drove here today without Java, and I made it without having to pull over once." His voice sounded confident and strong. He seemed proud of his progress, which was such a good sign. So far Luke had hit all the marks.

He *was* proud of himself, she realized. And she was as well. All the hard work paid off over time, and she was glad that Luke was able to appreciate the strides he was making without her having to point them out.

"That's huge," Destiny said. "All of these forward steps add up."

"They sure do," he acknowledged. "I can feel it. Even if I falter along the way, I'm still moving forward."

She began lightly clapping her hands together, feeling joyful. "That's just what I like to hear. Why don't we work outside today? The festival is a few days away, so it's also great preparation for that."

So far they had been working inside the barn almost exclusively. With lots of dogs running around the property, it would be a great way to reinforce Java's focus on Luke and his needs. Even though Luke hadn't confirmed his attendance at the event, Destiny had a lot of faith that he would show up. He was a highly motivated handler.

"I like that idea," Luke said, his face lighting up with a huge smile. He bent down and patted Java. "How about it, girl? Ready to be outside in this glorious Alaskan weather? You were born for this."

"You've got that right. Like most huskies, she adores being outside. The Alaskan climate is perfect for her."

Alaskan husky dogs, known for their resilience and hardworking natures, were indigenous to Alaska. Because of their strong work ethic, they were also used as Iditarod sled dogs. They had always been a personal favorite of hers.

The weather was brisk with a storm front coming later this afternoon that would bring several inches of rain to the region. Late September was the most unpredictable month of all in Alaska, with sun, snow, rain and even the occasional big snow event.

"I have to admit that I missed this climate. Being overseas in places like Cameroon and Iraq was pretty mind blowing. I'm not used to extreme heat."

Destiny shook her head. "Me neither. I can't even imagine being that hot."

"Have you traveled much outside of this area?" he asked conversationally as they walked toward the fenced in area.

"Not a whole lot. I went to Europe and I've traveled to Nashville with some friends." As soon as the words came tumbling off her lips, Destiny stiffened up. She tried her best never to bring up that awful trip to Nashville. It had sent her life into a tailspin and left her with unimaginable trauma. If only she could go back in time and never get on the plane.

"Judging by the look on your face, Nashville wasn't a hit," Luke remarked, looking over at her. Her heartbeat increased and she found herself tongue tied.

"I—I just think it was too crowded for my liking," she said, stumbling over her words. "I prefer wide-open spaces."

"Amen to that," Luke said, nodding his head. "We're blessed to live in this spectacular place."

"So, I meant to ask you how it went at Humbled with Java," she said, quickly changing the subject. "When I ran into you, everything seemed to be going smoothly. Were there any challenges?"

"It went really well. No one asked if they could pet her, so that's something I'd like to work on in the event that it happens. I want to be able to handle it in the right way."

"Okay, why don't we do some role-playing. You can use some of the commands you've learned with Java, and then I'll approach asking to pet her." They were now on the other side of the barn, where Java wouldn't be distracted by the other canines.

"Sounds good," Luke said, leading Java by her leash. "From our lessons I know there are several ways to handle it."

"If she has the red service vest on that's going to be straightforward," Destiny said.

"I can simply say she's a service dog in training and she can't be distracted."

"Absolutely," she said, encouraged that he had absorbed so much information from their training sessions.

They went over different scenarios, with Luke gaining more confidence with each effort. He really was an excellent student, and in a matter of weeks he would be graduating from the program, and Java would live with him full-time. Thankfully, Java was already an experienced service dog, which cut down the number of skills she needed to learn. They worked for the rest of the lesson on positive reinforcement, with Java being the recipient of numerous bacon-flavored treats.

Destiny folded her arms across her chest and stood a distance away from Luke and Java, simply watching them. As Luke drew closer she said, "Java trusts you. That's a wonderful gift, and it bodes well for your future together."

She could tell that Luke was trying to play it cool, but his expression broke into a wide grin that threatened to take over his entire face. He placed his hand on his chest. "Aww, shucks. That means a lot to me."

Her thoughts were beginning to race a little bit with possibilities. Luke would be a great asset to her program. He was a quick learner, great with dogs and he had a compassionate spirit. She wondered if he might consider working with her.

She turned away from him, only to feel a whack against her shoulder blade. Destiny whirled around. She sputtered. "W-what was that?"

Luke was standing a few feet away from her, laughing so hard he was clutching his side. A huge smile appeared on his face. Luke clumsily tried to hide it with his hand.

"D-did you throw a snowball at me?" she asked, incredulous. It had been years since anyone had done so.

He lightly shrugged. "Maybe. Can you prove it?" he asked, trying to keep a straight face.

"Seriously? I should have known this was coming. You were always a sneaky snowball hurler when we were kids." She put her hands on her hips. "I see nothing has changed."

"You're right. And getting hit by a snowball still sends you into a tizzy, just like when we were kids." Luke was laughing so hard now he was almost breathless.

In an instant she reverted back to being an eight-year-old girl. While Luke was busy laughing, she bent over and scooped up a handful of snow, then shaped it into the perfect snowball. With impeccable aim, she hurled it at Luke, landing it on his chest. *Womp!* She grinned as it hit him, making a loud thumping sound.

"Hey!" Luke's voice was filled with mock outrage. "You hit me."

She grinned at him. "I sure did. You got exactly what you deserved." For good measure she put her thumb on her nose and made a face, fully reverting to her childhood self.

"Oh, you shouldn't have done that," Luke said, charging toward her with alarming speed. Java let out a bark and joined the chase.

Destiny squealed and began running in the opposite direction. She couldn't recall the last time she'd been so gleeful. Before she knew what was happening, Destiny was being lifted in the air by strong arms. Her feet dangled in the air and she kicked her legs in an attempt to break free. At this point she was giggling up a storm. Luke whirled her around, and in the process, lost his footing. They both tumbled to the ground, landing on soft patches of snow. Java began sniffing them in a protective manner, all of her K9 instincts on full alert but her tail wagging too.

"Oops," Luke said. "Are you all right?"

Destiny chuckled. "Are you kidding me? This isn't the first time I've gone down in a snowball fight."

"You always were right in the thick of things, even though you were two years younger than the rest of us." Something flared in Luke's eyes that looked like admiration.

"I never wanted to be left out," she said. "And thanks to you always having my back, I never was." Despite what he'd been through, she knew that Luke was still the person she'd grown up with—sweet, caring and disciplined.

Their eyes locked and held. There wasn't a single doubt in her mind as to what was coming. And she wanted this more than she'd ever wanted anything in her life. Everything slowed down as if the world was now moving in slow motion. Luke's lips brushed against hers—softly, tenderly—causing butterflies to flutter in her stomach. She pushed all of her caution aside and leaned into the kiss. As his lips moved over hers, she tasted cinnamon and vanilla. Pure sweetness.

She didn't shrink away from his touch or freeze up. Being in his arms felt so right. She felt safe and protected, something that she'd thought was a thing of the past. Everything felt so wonderful, like a new beginning.

She didn't want this moment to end, although she knew this wasn't the time or place to explore their connection. It would be mortifying if her next client came driving up and spotted them making out like two teenagers.

"That was nice," Luke murmured. "And unexpected."

"I'm not sure what Java makes of this," she teased. The husky was sitting a few feet away looking at them with her head cocked to the side.

She heard the low thrum of voices from the other side of the barn. Thankfully they couldn't be seen from over there. "I should head back for my next lesson." Luke stood up and held out his hand to her. She gripped his hand and he helped her to her feet.

"See you next time," Luke said, his eyes trained on her as she walked away.

It was getting more difficult to view Luke merely as a client and an old friend. He was burrowing himself more deeply into her world, and she found herself wanting to peel back all of her layers. She wanted Luke to truly see her. Destiny yearned to share the secret that she kept so closely guarded.

But would Luke view her differently if he discovered the secret she had been carrying around for the past three years? The question nagged at her as she walked back toward the barn with Java.

No, she couldn't go there, she decided. It was best to keep her guard up. Opening up to him was a risk that she wasn't willing to take.

Chapter Nine

Sharing a kiss with Destiny had been out of this world. He couldn't stop thinking about it, nor could he figure out if it had been the best or worst move of his life. Nothing had changed with his situation. He was still not the man she thought he was, and he wasn't worthy of a woman like her. He didn't deserve a happy ending, not when Rico and Tony were no longer a part of this world.

Yet, he'd made a move and kissed her. It had been a beautiful mistake.

Luke ran a shaky hand over his face. He really wanted a friend to serve as a sounding board, but discussing this with Charlie would be incredibly awkward. "Hey, I kissed your sister. Can I get some advice?" Right about now he really wished he had kept in contact with more of his local friends, like the Locke twins, Brody and Caden, as well as Ryan Campbell. If he hadn't kept himself as such a recluse, things might be different.

Rosie would probably jump for joy if he told her, but he wasn't going to divulge that type of information to her. It was all his sister would need in order to go full matchmaker on him. His big sister wouldn't hesitate to put him and Destiny on the spot. That could be embarrassing for both of them. He wondered if she was projecting on to him because of her fractured relationship with Jake.

This afternoon was the Alaskan Moon festival, and Rosie had called him half a dozen times, asking if he was attending. The truth was, he still hadn't made up his mind. His computer dinged, alerting him to new messages. After taking a fortifying breath, Luke opened the latest message he'd received from Anita. He was practically gritting his teeth, but he knew that in order to move on he had to face this head on.

Luke, I hope that life is treating you well. I've reached out to you a few times with no response. I imagine it's been difficult for you to rebuild your life. I would love to talk to you about Rico's passing since you're the only person I can ask. I would like closure so I can start to move past this. Would love to hear from you.

God bless,
Anita

Luke groaned. Why had he opened up the email? He wouldn't be able to get her words out of his mind now. Anita was a good woman who'd been a wonderful mother to Rico. Her grief must be profound. Being the mother of a Navy SEAL involved constant worry and stress.

Tony's wife, Nadia, had been an amazing partner to his friend. The divorce rate for SEALs was extremely high. From what Luke had observed, they had been a dedicated and loving couple.

On impulse, Luke made the decision to attend the Alaskan Moon festival. It would be a wonderful diversion from the situation with Rico's mother. He didn't need to feel any more guilt. He was already drowning in it. While getting ready for the event, he spent way too much time deciding what to wear. Since he'd never really worried about his physical appearance, Luke knew on some level he wanted to look good for Destiny. He didn't know how she felt about him, other than his belief that they had chemistry and appreciated each other's company.

And that soul-soaring kiss they'd shared! That spoke volumes as far as he was concerned.

He sent a quick text to Destiny confirming his presence at the event.

I'm coming to the festival.

A few dots appeared on his screen followed by the word Squee and a celebratory emoji.

I was hoping you would come. I'm headed over shortly with Java.

Let's meet up. How about the town green?

That works for me. How about noon?

See you then.

He put his phone away, feeling practically giddy. Having the ability to actually make plans with someone and be able to drive with a measure of confidence lifted him to the stratosphere.

Once he arrived in the downtown area and parked his truck, nerves began to take over.

Luke wasn't sure if he'd made the right decision about attending the Alaskan Moon festival. Then again, his goal in training with Java was to make progress, and this was part of it. The large number of townsfolk milling about Main Street caused him to second-guess himself. Could he really do this?

As someone who'd been hiding out for the past year, being out in the open at a town festival was a bit overwhelming. "Just breathe," he said out loud, quickly noticing the surprised looks of many townsfolk as he walked past them. "And so it begins," he muttered as one of his mother's friends approached him. For the next few minutes, Luke did his best to keep a smile on his face as he answered all of her questions. His stomach was tied up in knots. Clearly his parents hadn't told many people about his being home. He had to wonder if they were ashamed of him no longer being a SEAL and having PTSD. That being said, Luke hadn't wanted his presence in town to be known, so he couldn't really be upset about his folks keeping quiet about it.

It seemed that every step he took, another familiar face would stop him and pepper him with questions. He did his best to keep his cool, explaining that he was no longer deployed as a SEAL but not giving any additional details. For the most part, no one pressed him for further details although several seemed shocked.

Needing a break, Luke stood out of view behind a store's awning. He blew out a deep breath and tried to collect himself.

"Luke! Is that you?" The raspy voice was instantly recognizable. Caden Locke, one of his oldest friends, was standing a few feet away from him. He had just stepped out of a general store. Caden's jaw was practically hanging open.

"Caden," Luke said, surprise registering in his voice.

As much as he hadn't been prepared to come face-to-face with his old friend, Luke was happy to see him. Luke was instantly swept up into a bear hug. Tall and broad shouldered, Caden had always been athletic, along with his twin brother, Brody. Now a pilot, Caden had a thriving business flying folks in and out of Serenity Peak. He was living out his childhood dreams, and Luke couldn't be more proud of him.

"When did you get back?" Caden asked. "I had no idea."

"Honestly, I've been back for a while," he admitted. It felt good to finally be able to speak the truth.

"Seriously?" Caden asked. "I had no idea. Why didn't you reach out?"

"It's a long story, but I'm not a SEAL anymore. I've been really going through it as a result of something that happened over in Africa." He made a face. "Maybe another time we can sit down and I can tell you all about it."

Caden's expression softened. "I'm so sorry to hear that. I'd really like to catch up, if you're up to it. Totally on your terms, buddy."

How could he have forgotten how empathetic Caden had always been? All this time he'd been hiding away from true friends who cared about him. He couldn't go back and change anything, but he could continue moving forward like Destiny suggested.

"Sounds like a plan," he said, grinning. He took out his cell phone and handed it to Caden. "Put your number in my contacts and we'll make it happen."

They parted ways after promising to get together within the next week.

He felt pure adrenaline racing through his veins as he began walking quickly toward the meetup spot he'd arranged with Destiny. So far, today was proving that he could handle difficult situations that up until this point had unnerved him.

He couldn't help but link all of his progress to the day Destiny had come back into his life.

Destiny couldn't explain the feeling of anticipation coursing through her as she waited by the snowy town green for Luke. Despite the chill, her palms were moist and she felt a little warm. It was almost like that first-day-of-school feeling, when nerves and excitement were all jumbled up together. Java seemed to sense something in the air as well. Perhaps she was picking up on Destiny's emotions. The Husky seemed to be on high alert, her ears perked up and a look of intensity on her sweet face. It was almost as if the pup was looking for Luke in the crowd of people.

All of a sudden Destiny spotted Luke walking toward the town green. She sucked in a little breath at the sight of him. He looked better than ever in a navy parka and dark washed jeans. The closer he got to them, the more excited Java became. Her tail was wagging so hard Destiny thought it might just fall off. It was a credit to the fact that she was well trained that she didn't break away from Destiny and run toward Luke, even though she knew the Husky wanted nothing more in this world.

"Hey," Luke said as he reached their side. "Good to see you," he said, all smiles as he leaned down and lavished some attention on Java, who was soaking it up like a plant needing sunshine.

"Thanks for coming," Destiny said. "I honestly wasn't sure I'd see you here until you sent that text."

Luke shoved his hands into his back pockets. "I didn't want to confirm until I was absolutely sure that I was going to make it."

"Well, I'm thrilled you decided to come," she told him. "I think you'll find that being here with all of the crowds is a good litmus test."

"My being here is already raising some eyebrows," Luke said, looking around him. He made a face. "I've been stared at and peppered with questions since my arrival."

Destiny had immediately noticed all of the gawking and stares. Not a single person was being subtle. She couldn't imagine how annoyed Luke must feel. This was the very thing he'd been worried about.

Destiny sighed. "I'm sorry about all the stares and questions. It's amazing how rude folks can be." Serenity Peak was a small Alaskan town, but the gossip mill could be brutal. She imagined that the sight of Luke was causing tongues to wag. Enough people in town knew he'd been back for some time to wonder why he was no longer deployed as a SEAL. Not to mention why he'd been tucked away and out of sight.

"It's not your fault. For the most part it's been fine, but it might get a bit old by the end of the event."

Destiny nodded. "I get it. You're still not ready to be put under the spotlight. Why don't you take Java and we can start putting into practice some of the things you've been learning."

"Sounds good to me," Luke said as Destiny handed him

Java's leash. In her red service vest the husky looked perky and professional.

"I'll walk behind you and observe," Destiny said. "If you have to stop and talk to someone, just make sure you give Java the proper commands so she sits beside you."

Luke began walking with Java, who was totally in tune with him as her handler. Destiny stood at a discreet distance each time Luke was stopped by people wanting to talk. She could tell he was fielding questions by the way his body shifted uncomfortably. At other times he also seemed genuinely happy to be reconnecting with a few folks.

"Did you notice how Java stepped between you and Ralph? She sensed your stress and wanted to separate you from that particular situation."

A look of comprehension passed over Luke's face. "What a smart girl she is. I wasn't sure about what she was doing. She was so discreet." He dug into the treat pouch and pulled out a pumpkin-flavored snack for Java. "Way to go, Java," he said, giving her the positive reinforcement she so deserved.

"How did it feel?" Destiny asked, hoping that handling Java in this crowded venue bolstered his self-assurance.

"To be completely honest, it was an incredibly natural feeling. Java makes everything better. She gives me courage," he said, a smile tugging at his lips.

In this moment Destiny couldn't ask for more. Her heart was full. Watching Luke soar with confidence was incredible to witness.

The smell of grilled seafood and burgers wafted in the air, causing Destiny's stomach to growl. She'd been so excited about the festival she hadn't eaten all day.

"Hungry?" Luke asked with a grin. "I could eat something too if you're game."

She was happy to see that the townsfolk's' focus on his presence at the festival hadn't dampened his spirits. Or his hunger. "I'm starving," she admitted. "We could grab a bite from one of the food trucks or stands unless sitting down at a restaurant appeals to you."

"The food trucks are so amazing this year. I'd love to check them out," Luke said, "and it might be easier, since Java is with us."

"Good point, although with her service vest on, she's welcome at most town establishments," Destiny reminded him. Accommodating handlers and their service dogs was an important issue. Knowing this, would give Luke the freedom to bring Java along with him on outings.

Luke nodded. "Got it."

As they passed a seafood stand, Luke stopped and rubbed his stomach. "Check out this menu. Crab legs. Seafood chowder. Teriyaki salmon bites. Rosemary fries. Everything looks good."

"It really does," she said. "I'm also eyeing the gyro truck. They're my all-time favorites."

"Why don't I order a few things from here while you do the same at the gyro truck. Best of both worlds, right?" he asked.

"I like your style," she said, giving him a thumbs-up. She began walking toward the gyro truck, her appetite increasing with every step.

After ordering the food and waiting for it to be prepared, Destiny headed back toward Luke. He had a look of strain etched on his face, with creases on his forehead and little lines around his mouth. He was radiating an aura of stress as he talked to a few of the townsfolk. She found herself frowning as she approached them.

"Afternoon, ladies. Sorry to interrupt," she said, "but we don't want this food to get cold." She held up the platter as proof.

The two older women—the Parker sisters—looked disappointed at the interruption. "What a shame," Dot said. "We so love talking to you, Luke."

"It's not every day we get to see a real live hero," Laura gushed, reaching out and touching Luke's arm.

Destiny made eye contact with Luke, letting him know that he could say his goodbyes and walk off with her. Luke seemed almost glued to the spot against his will.

"Nice to see you, ladies," Luke said with a forced smile. He walked away with her as they headed to the tented seating area. Destiny headed toward a secluded table, suspecting that Luke wouldn't want any more prying eyes.

Once they sat down, Luke didn't waste any time unwrapping his food and digging in to his salmon bites. He paused to pull a can of soda from each of his pockets and slid one over to Destiny.

"I hope you still like root beer," Luke said.

Destiny let out a little squeal of excitement. Sometimes it was the little things that meant the most. "Oh, what a treat. I love root beer. Thanks for remembering."

He nodded. "Some things we never forget. I remember how Charlie would always pick you up a can at the general store."

The memory washed over her like a warm rain, reminding her of her wonderful childhood. She'd been blessed to have a brother as amazing as Charlie.

Destiny was pulled out of her thoughts by Luke's awkward posture. He still seemed a little stiff and not completely relaxed. "Is everything all right? You looked a bit uncomfortable back there with the Parkers."

He swung his gaze up from focusing on his plate to meet her own. "I'm fine. It's just a lot all at once." He shifted uncomfortably in his seat. "It's sensory overload. For so long I've been away from town events and large groups of people. Reintegrating myself into the fabric of this town will take some time."

Destiny bit her lip. Maybe Luke hadn't been ready for this excursion. "I'm sorry, Luke. I shouldn't have pushed you so hard out of your comfort zone."

"No, please don't blame yourself. I'm enjoying myself and feeling much more comfortable in a crowded setting because Java is with me. Maybe I just need to be better at boundaries."

"What do you mean?" she asked, feeling curious.

"A lot of folks ask probing questions about why I'm no longer deployed. I need to get more comfortable with letting them know I'm not ready to talk about it yet."

Destiny took a big bite of her gyro, then washed it down with her soda. "Yes, that's a great point. It's not healthy for you to allow others to push past those boundaries. And it should be enough for them to hear those words from you and stop pressing."

They ate in companionable silence with Java lying down peacefully next to Luke. The husky very clearly saw him as her handler now. Java was already showing signs of being hopelessly devoted to Luke. This was one of the foundations for a great handler-service dog relationship. Score! They'd put in the work to be a success story.

Once they were done eating, they got back to it, with

Luke taking Java to an area with noisy kids and loud noises. Luke calmly gave the pup commands, and she dutifully obeyed them all. From everything she was witnessing, Luke and Java were ready to graduate from her program. Since Java had already spent years in service training, her experience had helped immeasurably.

The sounds of jazz music filled the air, and as they walked farther down Main Street they came across a band and a makeshift dance floor. Charlie was out there cutting a rug, and when he spotted the two of them, he beckoned them to join him. Luke pointed toward Java and shrugged. She knew he'd found the perfect excuse not to dance. She didn't blame him one bit, since that would only increase the number of people staring at him. As it was, Destiny had the feeling that folks were looking at the two of them and wondering if they were an item. That was how small towns worked.

"Let's go check out the games," Luke suggested, pointing toward the area where the carnival games were. There were so many—corn hole, guessing games, the water gun race and balloon darts. Kids with cotton candy were milling about and trying to win prizes. She felt a rush of excitement at the prospect of taking home a stuffed animal as a prize.

"Isn't that teddy bear sweet?" she asked, pointing toward one of the prizes hanging above the balloon darts. She dug in her pocket and pulled out a few dollar bills. "I'm going to try," she said, handing her money over to the person manning the booth.

"I'm rooting for you," Luke called from behind her as she stepped up to the counter and began playing the game.

Time after time Destiny lost to another player. Something told her that this wasn't her game. "Oh well," she said, turning back toward Luke, "it wasn't meant to be."

"Mind if I give it a whirl?" he asked.

"Go for it," she said. "It's not as easy as it looks."

The other people playing groaned as soon as Luke stepped up to play, no doubt figuring he was a ringer with his rugged physique.

On his first go-round, Luke won. And he continued his winning streak for five rounds, earning himself a prize. The kid manning the booth told him to pick whatever he wanted. She watched as he selected the teddy bear she'd been admiring.

"Here you go," he said, offering her the bear.

"Luke, that's so sweet of you," she said, immediately pressing the stuffed animal against her chest. They walked away from the games and toward the library, pausing by the steps.

"It's the least I could do," he drawled. "For the many things you've done for me."

"You deserve to get your life back, Luke. And I'm proud to be just a small part of that journey." She felt emotional, thinking of all the work he'd done to reclaim his life.

And at the same time, he'd helped her as well—and he didn't even know it. Because of him she now knew that she could trust a man. She could be kissed by a man without flinching. Even now, she was alone with him in a more secluded area and her thoughts were calm.

His brown eyes met her own. A look of longing radiated from his eyes, mirroring her own feelings. This might not be the time or place, but she wanted to kiss this man. He leaned down and brushed his lips against hers. Butterflies fluttered in her stomach all over again. She leaned against him, returning his kiss with equal measure.

Destiny stood on her tiptoes, one hand clutching the lapels of his jacket for leverage while the other held on to the stuffed bear. As Luke's lips moved over her own, everything else faded away until it seemed as if it was just the two of them. The kiss was full of so much tenderness that it healed something inside of her that had been ripped apart three years ago. With every kiss from Luke, she was being restored.

"Luke," she whispered against his lips. As they pulled apart, Luke grazed his knuckles against her cheek. The low rumble of voices caused them to move a discreet distance away from one another as a crowd of kids passed by the library steps.

One thing was for certain. She was in over her head with Luke. Kissing him didn't feel casual or insignificant. After what she'd been through, it was monumental. He was breaking down her walls at a fast rate. Destiny knew that if she was going to move forward with Luke, she would have to tell him about the devastating assault that had turned her world upside down.

Chapter Ten

W̲alking around the festival with Destiny by his side made Luke feel more content than he'd been in ages. There wasn't any doubt in his mind that she was the source of his new-found contentment, along with the best service dog in the world. Destiny's encouragement and belief in him had changed his world for the better as well as his outlook. Because of her, he wanted to keep pushing past his comfort zone and live life to the fullest, as he'd done before the explosion.

Amidst the jubilant feelings, Luke was nervous. He was still carrying around this awful weight that he couldn't seem to get rid of. He wasn't prepared to fall in love, even though all the signs were there. On a gut level Luke knew that he was falling in love with Destiny. Stopping these emotions would be like trying to stop a freight train by placing a feather in its path.

Ahead, he spotted Charlie and Caden in a group that included some of their childhood friends—Caden's twin brother, Brody, and their pal Ryan Campbell.

"Hey, Luke," Charlie greeted him before turning to his sister and Java. "Great to see you guys here." Java, recognizing him, began to wag her tail and pant with excitement.

"Hey," Luke said, greeting everyone. "It's great to see everyone."

"I'm going to go talk to Molly while you guys catch up," Destiny said before walking off with Java. He could see Molly in the distance at the game area.

A little kernel of nervousness twisted in his gut at being left alone with the group. Java wasn't the only one he leaned on. Destiny's presence always made him feel more centered. He hadn't seen his friends in years. He had so much to explain to them it felt overwhelming.

"We just heard you were back," Ryan said, slapping him on the shoulder. "Where have you been?"

Luke exchanged a glance with Charlie, who'd known about his presence in town this entire time, as well as about the explosion. Charlie nodded at him encouragingly, letting him know he should talk to his friends.

He let out a ragged breath. "I'm sorry that I didn't reach out, but I came back home after a traumatic event overseas." He quickly caught them up to speed on the explosion. Luke steeled himself and took a steadying breath before continuing. "Two of my SEAL buddies passed away as a result of their injuries. As a result, I suffer from PTSD. Seeing my team members die such a horrific way broke something inside of me."

Brody stepped toward him. "I'm so sorry, Luke. I can't imagine what you went through. It's so tragic."

"We're here for you," Ryan said. "Every step of the way."

"Whatever you need," Caden said. "We've got your back."

Just hearing his friends voice their support meant everything to him. All this time he'd been consumed by thoughts of being judged, but he couldn't have been more wrong.

"What Luke forgot to say is that he's training with Java as part of his PTSD," Charlie added. "And from what I hear, he's a star pupil."

"That's great," Caden said. "Destiny's K9 farm has gotten great word of mouth."

"Why don't we plan a night out at Northern Lights?" Charlie suggested. "Let's put something on the calendar."

"Definitely," Ryan said. "I can't wait to tell you about getting married to Skye, and about my daughter. A lot has changed in Serenity Peak."

"Sounds like a plan," Luke said, firm in the knowledge that he now had the strength to drive into town and go to public places without having a panic attack. And, he could always bring Java along with him for support. It was amazing how much things had improved in the past few weeks.

"You're a hero," Ryan said with a nod. "We want to celebrate you."

"Yes," Brody chimed in. "We're proud of you. And so is Serenity Peak."

"We should organize a town parade in your honor," Caden said, looking around at the group for encouragement. Suddenly, everyone was nodding and agreeing with Caden. Their features were animated. His heart sank.

At the moment, he couldn't feel any more like a fraud. A town parade in his honor? That would be outrageous. There was no way he could allow that to happen, especially knowing what he knew.

Just then Destiny walked back over and said, "Sorry to interrupt, but it's time to get back to it. Java's getting a little antsy."

Relief flooded him. He said his goodbyes to the group, trying to seem upbeat even though he was crumbling on the inside. As they walked away, he noticed Charlie was looking at him and Destiny in a questioning way. Was he sensing the deepening connection between them? And, if so, did he approve?

Hero. The word was racing around in his head. His heart was thumping, pulse racing. He felt as if he were in a pressure cooker. Something had to give. He was on the verge of imploding. Luke couldn't even count the number of times he'd been called a hero today.

Luke began praying for some sort of release from this feeling of being a fraud. He couldn't deal with it a minute longer. It was too much for him to bear.

He could feel Destiny's gaze on him like laser beams. Luke knew she meant well, but it only intensified the pressure he was under.

"What happened back there? Did someone say something?" Destiny asked. Her features were creased with worry. He hated making her feel this way. She was the type of person who should only experience love and light.

He ran a hand over his face. "Yes, they were calling me a hero. Over and over again." He let out a tortured groan. "It's been happening all day."

"And that bothers you?" Her voice sounded incredulous.

"Yes, it does," he said through clenched teeth.

"You should be proud of your service. You *are* a hero."

As soon as the words reached his ears, something inside of him cracked wide-open. So many people viewed him as heroic and noble. It was a lie. And he couldn't do it anymore. He didn't deserve all of the accolades and support. White-hot anger flowed through him, throwing him off-kilter and spoiling the upbeat mood between him and Destiny.

He turned to face her, stopping in his tracks. She must've seen something in his expression because she stopped walking as well.

"No, Destiny. You're wrong. I'm the furthest thing from a hero," he told her. Just hearing her utter the *H* word made him feel unworthy. He wasn't anybody's hero. And it made his insides twist to hear Destiny call him one. He should have set her straight weeks ago, so she didn't harbor these illusions.

"What are you talking about?" she scoffed. "You've done incredible things as a SEAL. Heroic things that most people can only dream about doing."

He vigorously shook his head and took a step backward.

"Luke, what is it? What's going on? Why are you acting like this?"

"Because it was all my fault. If it hadn't been for my mistake, Tony and Rico would still be alive. That's my reality and what I live with each and every day. They're dead because of me!"

"I can't be here right now," he said, handing Destiny Java's leash and storming away from her, his movements full of intensity.

Was this really happening right now? Everything had been going so well.

"Luke! Come back. Wait!" Try as she might, her legs couldn't keep up with Luke's powerful strides. She stopped walking, choosing instead to think about what Luke had just said to her. It made no sense whatsoever.

What had Luke meant when he'd told her that he was responsible for the deaths of his Navy Seal comrades? Perhaps this was part of his PTSD. She'd heard of a condition called survivor's guilt—it happened when people who lived through a tragic event felt guilty for being alive when others had perished.

There was no point in looking for him. He was gone, swallowed up by the crowd. She tried her best to find him, but Destiny couldn't spot him anywhere. Would he have left the event without telling her goodbye? Their time together had been playful and romantic until a few remarks had thrown Luke off-kilter. She dialed his cell phone several times, praying he would pick up her call.

She made her way through the crowd, hoping to catch a glimpse of Luke. Maybe he'd simply needed a few moments to himself. Suddenly, she spotted Charlie in the crowd. She quickly made her way over to him.

"Charlie, have you seen Luke?" she asked, feeling frantic.

"Not recently." He frowned at her. "Slow down, Destiny. Take a deep breath."

"I don't have time for that," she said, knowing she looked and sounded flustered. "I need to make sure he's okay."

"What's going on? He seemed fine a little while ago."

"He wasn't fine, Charlie. Not in the slightest." Her voice cracked with emotion.

"Is there something going on between the two of you that I should know about?" Charlie asked in a disapproving tone.

"No," she snapped. "Nothing you should know about."

Charlie frowned. "Look, I know he's your client, but it's not your responsibility to take care of him."

She was taken aback by how cold her brother sounded. What was going on with him? Hadn't he always been the one who would lend a helping hand to someone in need? Luke was his closest friend.

"He's your friend too, Charlie." She could hear the hurt ringing out in her voice. "He's been through something very traumatic." She bit down on her back teeth. "I know what that's like."

His features softened. "I know. He's my best friend, Destiny. I care about him too."

"Then act like it," she snapped. "If the situation was reversed, Luke would be all in for you."

"Luke is important to me, but *you're* my sister. It's my job to make sure *you're* okay first. *You're* my priority."

"I'm fine. But Luke isn't. And for the record, I'm not some fragile doll that you have to protect because of what happened to me."

"I know you're not," Charlie said, holding up his hands. "You're the strongest person I know."

"Then trust me on this," Destiny implored him. On some level she was testing their relationship. She'd leaned on Charlie tremendously over the past few years, and maybe because of that, he continued to treat her like a baby sister rather than a grown woman.

"I'm just asking you to stay and enjoy the festival. Luke will cool down if you give him space." Charlie looked a bit sheepish, as if he knew he'd been a bit disloyal to his best friend. She appreciated him looking out for her, but not at Luke's expense.

"I'm going after him," she told Charlie. She didn't need her brother's permission to go after someone she cared about.

Rather than argue the point, Charlie simply nodded. "Keep me posted. Luke's my best friend and I love him, but I'm worried that you might be in over your head."

Although she appreciated the fact that he cared about

her well-being, Luke's situation wasn't going to derail any of the progress she'd made over the past three years. Being there for Luke was separate from her own issues.

"I really have to go. I'll call you," she said. She could feel Charlie's eyes trailing after her as she trudged toward the lot. Once she put Java in the truck, she got behind the wheel and made one last attempt to reach out to Luke by phone.

Why wasn't he answering? Now her worry had ratcheted up a few notches. What if he'd been so upset he had gotten into an accident?

Dear Lord, please watch over Luke. He's been through so much. Keep him safe in the palm of Your hand.

On the way to Luke's property she kept her eyes peeled for any signs of his truck.

Thankfully it didn't appear that he'd been involved in an accident. The sun went down as she was driving, creating a beautiful visual that she normally enjoyed. The sky was a vivid orange with glimmers of yellow. Her nerves were too on edge to fully appreciate the Alaskan sunset. Luke's house was dark when she pulled into the driveway. Destiny got out of the truck, then commanded Java to jump down. With Java at her side, they looked around the property. Luke's truck was here so he had to be around somewhere. She saw a light glimmering inside the shed next door to the house. The first time she'd come here, that was where he'd been.

"Come on, Java. Let's go find Luke." Java seemed to understand her, because the pup raced toward the shed.

As soon as she pushed the door open, a stunning array of artwork came into view. An entire collection. Her gaze swung around to all of the pieces on display. There were oil paintings, watercolors, charcoal sketches. Some were works in progress, while others looked like finished pieces. Luke was standing by an easel with a paintbrush in his hand, decorating the canvas with bold strokes.

He turned toward her with a look of surprise stamped on his face. "Destiny. I didn't hear you drive up."

"I'm sorry for just barging in, but I've been looking all over for you," she explained.

"No worries," he said, putting his paintbrush down. "I should have said goodbye to you rather than just taking off."

"Luke. These are incredible!" she gushed, overwhelmed by what he'd created. Destiny wanted to keep her focus on Luke and his state of mind, but the paintings were breathtaking.

"Thanks. Just a hobby I do in my downtime," he explained. "It's a great therapy for my PTSD. It gives me a chance to focus my energies on the canvas."

"Looks like more than a hobby," she observed. "These are gallery worthy. You're very talented."

Luke scoffed. "Thanks, but I'm not trying to be the next Basquiat. I'm simply content to have a creative outlet."

"Well, I wanted to make sure that you were okay. The way you left… I was worried about you."

"You shouldn't have followed me. I know how much you were looking forward to the festival." He let out a frustrated sound. "I'm sorry about the way I left." Luke twisted his mouth. "I promised myself I wouldn't do that again after that first day at your farm."

"It's all right. I didn't mean to push any buttons."

"It's not your fault. There was just a lot going on. PTSD strikes when you least expect it."

"Luke, I have to ask. What did you mean when you said

it was your fault that Tony and Rico died?" The question had been burning inside her for the past hour.

As soon as the words left her mouth, tension hung thickly in the air. Luke's features tightened and a vein jumped around on his temple.

"Destiny, I don't want you to think badly of me."

She reached out and gripped his hand. "I wouldn't. It's not possible," she said. And she meant it. Luke was becoming so dear to her, and she thought the world of him. She truly couldn't imagine seeing him as anything other than a good man. A courageous one.

Her heart began to pound wildly. *What kind of awful secret was he keeping?*

"Talk to me. Please," she begged. Some instinct was telling her that it was important—not for her but for Luke.

"You have no idea how badly this is eating me up inside." His eyes were full of the rawest pain she'd ever seen.

All she wanted to do was take away his torment, even if it meant she needed to peel back her own layers in the process. "I do know, Luke. I've endured something traumatic myself, and for a long time I couldn't function. I could barely breathe."

Luke heard the sincerity ringing out in Destiny's voice. He ached for whatever she'd gone through that had brought trauma into her world. She was such a source of sunshine and inspiration. It was hard to believe she'd endured anything horrific because of the positive energy she exuded. But maybe that was part of her being so special.

He trusted her in a way he no longer allowed himself to believe in people. Maybe it was their shared past or perhaps it was all the help she had given him with her program and pairing him up with Java.

"Why don't we sit down?" he suggested, pointing her toward one of his stools.

Destiny quickly sat while he grabbed his paintbrushes and placed them in a tray until he could later clean them. He walked over and sat on a stool next to Destiny. They were so close together that it felt incredibly intimate.

He locked gazes with her, intent on not avoiding eye contact, no matter how uncomfortable he felt. "What I said at the festival is true. Because of my mistake, my SEAL buddies died in the blast. That's what I've been holding on to for the last year."

Destiny frowned but continued listening to him without interrupting.

"The day that our Humvee was attacked, I was driving. We had instructions regarding the roads we needed to avoid on our way to deliver supplies in this particular village. It was all made very clear to me as the driver. There was a map with those roads marked out with a red pen." His entire body was shaking. Suddenly he was back there in that awful moment when his entire world had turned upside down. "I can't remember exactly what happened, but I must've taken the wrong turn because our Humvee hit an IED. I messed up."

"Everyone makes mistakes," Destiny said in a soft voice. "We're human."

Luke understood what Destiny was trying to say, but he couldn't let himself off the hook so easily. "But mine cost two fine men their lives. That's more than a mistake. It was negligent."

"You blame yourself. Is that why you're not a SEAL

anymore?" she asked. Destiny was leaning toward him, her body language showing her keen interest in his story.

"In part," he admitted. "But the PTSD was my motivating factor. It would have been nearly impossible to perform at that high level while suffering from emotional trauma."

"That's understandable. You've been through a lot."

He nodded. That was an understatement. Watching two of his SEAL buddies die had torpedoed him in every way imaginable. "So you see, when people call me a hero, I want to scream at the top of my lungs. And tonight it all became too much for me to handle." He made a face. "At one point it felt like steam was coming out of my ears."

She reached out and gripped his forearm. "Luke, one mistake doesn't take away from everything you achieved in your career. You can still be considered a hero for all that you did prior to that horrible day. You've saved countless lives and performed amazing acts of courage. Don't minimize your service."

Just being supported by Destiny lifted his spirits. She was reminding him of things he'd chosen not to think about. Maybe she was right. One awful day didn't erase what came before it.

"I tend not to focus on before the explosion, but you're right. My SEAL career had been full of successful missions." He steepled his hands in front of him. "The thing is, I carry this around my neck like an anchor. It's become the one constant in my life, even though I wish it wouldn't be."

"I'm no expert, but it sounds like survivor's guilt. You're finding it hard to forgive yourself because you survived and they didn't."

Survivor's guilt. It was a term he'd heard of before in the SEAL community over the years and during his time in therapy. He understood the concept on a basic level but he hadn't really dug into it with his therapist. What Destiny had just said was making him think about his situation. Was this what he'd been suffering from all this time? If anyone but Destiny had spoken those words to him, Luke probably would have discounted them, but Destiny had proven to be a great source of support and information. He trusted her implicitly.

"Luke, it all sounds very jumbled in your mind. If chunks of time are missing, that means your memory of the event might be flawed."

"That's true," Luke said, letting out a ragged sigh. "It's frustrating to have those little gaps of time that I can't access. Sometimes I wonder if I'm suppressing those moments on purpose to spare myself the pain of reliving it."

"The bottom line is that we can't blame ourselves for things we don't have control over. You weren't the one who set off that bomb. Who's to say it wouldn't have happened if you'd taken those other routes?" She looked at him intensely. "Do you know that for a fact?"

He bit down on his back teeth. "No, I don't," he said, his mind whirling with questions. "Because everything happened at warp speed, I didn't ask a lot of questions. I was numb and in shock for weeks. And to this day I don't remember much about that day."

Destiny narrowed her gaze as she looked at him. "Well, it seems to me that you're placing this whole weight of responsibility on your shoulders without even having a clear overview of what exactly happened."

"I never thought of it in that way," he admitted. "I've been piecing things together from the fragments of memory I've held on to." He frowned. His thoughts were all over the place. Why hadn't he asked more questions before placing the blame solely on himself?

And now that he'd chosen to share his secret with Destiny, the ache inside of him was easing up. Had he known it would feel this good to unburden himself, he would have done it ages ago. Perhaps it had everything to do with the person he was confiding in. Every time he leaned on this woman, she proved to be as steady as a birch tree. He prayed that one day she would able to count on him for emotional support.

"Ultimately God is in control," Destiny said. "That's something you can't ever lose sight of."

Chapter Eleven

Luke. Sweet, amazing Luke.

The other night when they'd parted, Luke had seemed better than the way she found him. She was in awe of this man. He had bared his soul to her, peeling back his layers and showing her the parts of him he usually kept hidden. His courage was inspiring. The secret he'd been harboring had clearly been eating away at him. Believing he was culpable for the deaths of his two friends had placed him under extreme stress. On top of his PTSD, he'd been wrangling with this mountain of guilt.

Yet, he'd found the strength to tell her his truths.

At this point, how could she not do the same? They were very similar to each other, both of them hiding secrets from the world. She had almost told him about the assault last night, but truly the moment had been about Luke. In doing so she would have taken away the moment from him. She didn't want to do anything to derail his progress or halt his forward momentum.

He was perfectly imperfect. And she loved him for it.

It hit her all at once like being run over by a freight train. She was in love with Luke Adams. Truly, deeply in love. She didn't know where or when it had happened, but this feeling that had nestled itself inside of her wasn't like anything she had ever felt before.

She laughed giddily, overcome by the realization. She'd believed that the possibility of her falling in love with someone was one in a million. How many times had she vowed never to even look twice at a man? And now here she was, swept away by her handsome childhood friend. She knew that he still had a lot of healing to do, but she hoped to be by his side as he continued his journey. Did Luke share her feelings?

Her stomach was in knots, waiting for Luke and her other clients. They were set to practice for the showcase, which was less than a week away. She wanted everything to go as smoothly as possible. As a business owner, she still felt as if she were proving herself. A lot was riding on the showcase. In order to keep her program going, Destiny needed a steady stream of clients paying for her services. Although word of mouth was good, she needed folks to see the program's successes with their own eyes. Folks were coming to the showcase from neighboring towns, which was a big deal.

Buzz came ambling toward her with a few of her pups at his heels. "You look like a mama hen about to lay some eggs," he remarked, eyeing her shrewdly.

"Thanks for the compliment," she cracked. "I feel so special."

Buzz chuckled. "No offense meant, but you need to take some deep breaths. You've got this."

She immediately followed his advice by working on her breathing. "You're right. I just want to keep making forward strides. People need to see that this program is thriving." She chewed her lip.

"They will and they already do," Buzz said. "Every time I go into town that's all I hear about. Destiny's K9 farm is legendary."

Destiny beamed at her grandfather. "You just made my day."

He grinned back at her. "That's what grandpas are supposed to do."

"There's also the opportunity for a local investor." She rubbed her hands together. "Now, wouldn't that be wonderful?" The thought of Luke working alongside her at her K9 farm once again flitted through her mind. They made such a great team. Being a former Navy Seal, Luke would bring so many wonderful skills to the program.

"From your lips to God's ears, baby girl. I know how hard you've been working to grow your business," Buzz said, squinting into the distance. "Somebody's coming. Looks like Luke's truck if I'm not mistaken."

She turned her gaze toward the road, feeling euphoric at the sight of the Range Rover turning onto the property. She placed her hand on her midsection, willing the butterflies to settle down. "Luke," she said out loud, forgetting that her grandfather was standing beside her. Java, who knew Luke's truck on sight, trotted toward the driveway.

"I don't even need to ask," Buzz said, his eyes full of understanding. "It's written all over your face how you feel about that young man." He reached out and squeezed her hand. "If you ask me, I don't think you could have picked a finer fellow. He's top-notch." Buzz winked at her.

"Oh, Grandpa," she said, tears misting her eyes. His words were affirmations of her intense feelings about Luke. "I don't even know how he feels about me, so it might just be a whole lot of nothing." The very thought of her feelings not being reciprocated by Luke was painful. But she also knew that a few shared kisses didn't mean he wanted anything other than friendship between them.

"I can't imagine a savvy guy like Luke being so foolish," Buzz said, a fierce expression stamped on his face. Destiny laughed at his attempt to be intimidating. Everyone knew he was a teddy bear down to his core.

She leaned in and pressed a kiss to his cheek. "Aww. What would I do without you?"

Destiny didn't even want to think about losing him anytime soon.

When Luke got out of the truck, he began walking toward them, his hand raised in greeting. "Hey there. It's a beautiful day, considering there was a chance of snow."

The Alaskan sky was a robin's-egg blue color without a single snowflake in sight. It was a perfect day for setting up the showcase. Bright and beautiful.

"Luke! Great to see you," Buzz said, his voice bursting with cheerfulness.

"Hey, Luke. Thanks for being so prompt," Destiny said. "You're the first one to arrive."

"I'm going to head back inside and dabble around in the kitchen while a certain someone is otherwise occupied." Buzz jerked his head in her direction, leaving no doubt that he was talking about her. Luke chuckled as Buzz walked away.

"Don't encourage him," Destiny said, shaking her head. "He's such a character."

"That's why everyone loves him," Luke said, his lips twitching with merriment.

She didn't know if she was imagining it, but Luke appeared so much lighter, as if the weight of the world had been removed from his shoulders. Simply confiding his worst fears to another human being had done him a world of good.

There was something hovering in the air between them, a bond that had grown stronger since Luke's admission and their talk in his studio. She suspected that he felt it too.

"If I didn't say it enough the other night, I'm thankful for you. Not only did you listen to me, but you gave me things to think about," Luke told her. "Important things that have been helping me reframe the explosion. My guilt hasn't evaporated, but I'm beginning to question the actual facts as I've known them." He shrugged. "Or as I thought I did."

"I've been doing some research on survivor's guilt, and although my therapist mentioned it last year, I didn't really pay too much attention." He ran a hand across his jaw. "Honestly, maybe I wasn't ready to hear it back then."

She nodded. "You're at a different point in your journey, so that makes sense."

A smile played around his lips. "I am. I'm still dealing with the aftereffects of the explosion, but the past few mornings, when I woke up I wasn't blaming myself. Something shifted inside of me the other night and I owe it all to you."

"That makes me happy, but you're the one who's been doing all the heavy lifting. I think sometimes just giving voice to our burdens is healing." That was one of the reasons she wanted to tell all to Luke. How could he truly know her without knowing about her darkest moments?

"For a long time I thought telling anyone would make me feel more exposed, guiltier in some way if that makes sense. And honestly, I've worried about being judged. But that's not what happened. Confiding in you has lifted a tremendous burden off me." He squeezed her hand. "I don't feel so alone now."

Just hearing Luke give voice to these feelings caused a groundswell of emotion to rise up inside of her. They were good for one another. She could feel it in her bones.

"Thank you for trusting me," she said in a low voice. "It means the world to me."

"Thank you for listening. I hope you know that it wasn't just a random thing that it was you I confided in." His voice sounded strong, and he seemed more grounded today than before. It was as if something inside him had shifted after his revelation. "Ever since I started training with you, all you've shown me is grace and kindness." He reached out and swept his hand across her cheek. "You're some kind of wonderful, Destiny."

Her cheeks flushed at the compliment. Or was it Luke's tender touch that had sparked a reaction in her? At this point she couldn't tell, since his presence always turned her mind into mush.

"Right back atcha," she said, meeting his eyes despite her nervousness. Her heart was in her throat. Now that she'd realized the extent of her feelings for Luke, she couldn't help but wonder if she was wearing her emotions on her sleeve like a neon flashing sign. She had never been in love before. This was all new to her. It was such a beautiful feeling, yet her nerves were all over the place, wondering if he felt anything for her. Why hadn't anyone ever told her what this was like? Agony mixed with pure joy.

Vehicles began pulling up to the property, and Destiny waved as her other clients began to arrive. Just the sight of them caused a burst of pride to swell up in her chest. They, along with Luke, had worked incredibly hard to train with their individual service dogs. Their dedication and perseverance was awe-inspiring.

"There are things I'd like to say to you, but now probably isn't the best time," Luke said, looking around at the other people who'd just arrived at the property.

She nodded. "I understand. There are things I need to talk to you about too. There's something that I've kept secret from all but a few closest to me." She took a deep breath. "Your courage has inspired me to push past my fears, and that's an incredible feeling."

"Why don't we plan something just for the two of us?" Luke suggested, an easy smile spreading across his face. "No offense to Java, but she's kind of a third wheel."

Destiny burst out laughing. Come to think of it, the gorgeous husky had been with them one hundred percent of the way. It would be nice for just the two of them to spend time together. Even though what she had to tell him was heavy, she was looking forward to it. She trusted this man and wanted him to truly see her. Knowing what she'd been through would give him a brand-new perspective.

"Just tell me where and when," Destiny said. "I better go greet everyone so we can get started."

"I'll be right here with Java until you need me," Luke said. "Let me know if there's anything I can do to help out."

"I definitely will," she called out. There were some heavy boxes she needed moved from inside the barn.

As she walked away, Destiny put a little pep in her step. She couldn't remember a time when her spirts had been so high. Luke was giving off vibes that he wanted to step out of the friend zone with her. Things were looking up!

Soon there wouldn't be a single reason not to pursue a relationship with Luke.

* * *

Luke sat back and watched as Destiny organized the fenced-in area of the property for the showcase. With Isaac at her side, she was multitasking between the dogs, her clients and the props. He liked watching her. Luke enjoyed seeing the animated expressions on her face and the way she interacted with people. Everyone adored her. Like the sun, everything orbited around Destiny.

He spotted Thad from a distance with Lottie. The older man was waving wildly in his direction, and he grinned and waved back. Luke hadn't realized just how many clients Destiny worked with. More vehicles began pulling up, which meant more people and dogs. He shook his head. The place was a true dog farm, he thought. It brought a smile to his face, and he knew Destiny loved seeing all of her service dogs return for a visit. Like she always said, they were all just one big family.

Just as he was about to join the group, Charlie pulled into the driveway. As always, it was good to see his friend. He'd been so busy lately that they hadn't gotten together, but he was in a text group with Charlie, the Locke twins and Ryan where they were making plans for a meetup.

As soon as he stepped down from the truck, Charlie made a beeline in his direction. His long legs quickly carried him to where Luke was standing.

"Hey, Charlie. Are you joining in on the fun?" He knew how close Destiny and Charlie had always been. They had always supported one another in all of their endeavors.

Charlie held up a box with Humbled written on the side. "I'm bringing some croissants for Buzz. He sure has a sweet tooth," he said with a chuckle.

"Even when we were kids from what I recall," Luke said.

"He made the best chocolate chip cookies in the world. I couldn't get enough of those."

The memory settled over them like a warm fuzzy blanket. Their shared childhood had been filled with cozy remembrances like that one.

"Hey, buddy. Are you doing all right?" Charlie asked. "Destiny was really worried about you the other night at the festival."

"I'm good," he said, smiling at Charlie. It was amazing how much lighter he felt after divulging his secret to Destiny. He wasn't cured of his PTSD by any stretch of the imagination, but he wasn't entirely sure now that he'd been culpable for Tony's and Rico's deaths. He hadn't woken up this morning beating himself up for messing up the assignment and causing the deaths of two SEAL team members.

"You're finding it hard to forgive yourself because you survived and they didn't."

Destiny's words had penetrated his thoughts and made a huge difference in his outlook.

"Doing this service training program has made a world of difference. To be honest, I've been worried about this showcase and debating about whether I should pull out."

"You can't do that!" Charlie exclaimed in a raised voice. "Destiny would be crushed, Luke. She's counting on you."

"I know. It was just jitters. I owe you a debt of gratitude, friend. You're the one who steered me toward Destiny's K9 farm." He ran a hand over his jaw. "It's totally changed my world."

"I'm glad it's working out," Charlie said. A little frown sat on his forehead. "So, I noticed something at the festival. You and Destiny…there seems to be something going on between you." Charlie chewed his lip, an old habit from childhood. "Am I right?"

Luke didn't feel right talking about this with Charlie. Although they were close friends, he hadn't even discussed this subject with Destiny. He was still wrangling with his own feelings and trying to sort them out. He was falling for Destiny, but what came next? He had no idea, but in his heart, he wanted to be with her.

"There's not a whole lot I can say. It's something Destiny and I should talk about first, and we haven't as of yet." He looked his friend directly in the eyes. He was being as transparent as he could under the circumstances.

Charlie held up his hands. "Luke, I'm not trying to butt in. It's just that…she's been through a lot. It's not my place to say any more, but…please tread carefully with her. I'm worried you'll hurt her. She's clearly starting to lean on you."

Was Charlie alluding to the trauma Destiny had referenced the other night? He wasn't going to ask for any details, because he only wanted to know if Destiny told him herself.

"I would never do anything to hurt her," Luke said, feeling a little bit hurt that Charlie would believe him capable of harming his sister.

"I know you wouldn't do anything to cause her any pain. All I'm saying is be gentle. Be consistent. Don't back out of the showcase when she's counting on you." He shook his head. "I'm making a mess of this, and I'm sorry. I just had to say something." With those parting words Charlie headed off toward the house, leaving Luke baffled and completely bewildered. He hadn't given it too much thought before, but now he had to wonder if Charlie wasn't trying to run him off. Did he think Luke wasn't good enough to be with his baby sister? Or was he being sincere about his concerns?

No, he trusted Charlie. He'd never given him a reason to doubt him. Charlie's close bond with Destiny spoke volumes. Their whole lives Charlie had acted in the best interest of his sister. Luke had to believe that continued to be the case. His warning had sounded somber, but if Destiny had been treated poorly by a former boyfriend, that would explain Charlie's behavior. He was watching out for her. That wasn't about to happen with him.

"Luke!" Destiny called out as she headed toward him. "I was calling out to you. Didn't you hear me?"

He'd been so deep in thought that he must have blocked it out. Charlie had thrown him for a loop with his request.

"No, sorry about that," he apologized. "What's up?"

"I'm ready for you and Java. We're all going to line up and practice the procession." She squinted at him. "Are you sure you're okay? You were a million miles away just now."

That was another nice thing about Destiny being a part of his world. He always felt that she cared—deeply cared—about his well-being. Having someone like her in his corner made him feel as if he could climb mountains.

He put his game face on and flashed her a wide smile. For now, he was going to stuff down Charlie's concerns and be in the moment with Destiny. Charlie was simply being overprotective.

"I'm more than okay," he said, turning toward Java to make sure she was trailing after him as he walked side by side with Destiny. Faithful as ever, Java was trotting alongside him, looking up at him as if anticipating his every move. "That's a good girl, Java," he cooed.

This, he thought, was the type of peace he'd been seeking. Moments like this one had been few and far between since the nightmare overseas. He wasn't going to dwell on Charlie's none too subtle words of warning about being careful with Destiny.

Instead, he was going to seize the day with this wonderful woman he was falling in love with. And maybe, just maybe, he would summon the courage to tell her exactly how he felt about her.

Chapter Twelve

Destiny couldn't tamp down the rising tide of excitement she felt about the K9 showcase. Just seeing all of her past and present clients lined up and representing her service training program had been surreal and humbling. After everyone left, she'd taken a moment by herself to appreciate and reflect upon how far she'd come in three years. Back then she never would have envisioned owning a thriving K9 service training business. Nor would she have imagined reconnecting with Luke and falling head over heels in love with him.

God had been good to her. He had been her rock and foundation during the worst times of her life. At times her faith had wavered, but, in the end, Destiny had held on, firm in the knowledge that the dark times would pass.

Love. The emotion was nestled in her chest like a treasure she was keeping a secret from the rest of the world. It was a feeling that gave her wings and made her believe she could soar. All the books and the flowery poems were right. Love was healing the part of her that hadn't believed she could feel anything even remotely like this. Of course she'd been doing the work on recovering from her trauma for years, but Luke's presence in her life had done her a world of good. They'd helped each other, she thought, and that was a beautiful thing.

And now she was heading over to his place for dinner. She knew that this would be the time for her to talk about her past and the assault. Strangely, she didn't feel nervous. Luke had proven that he was a strong man of faith. He wouldn't disappoint her.

She had prepared a batch of double chocolate brownies to take over to Luke's for dessert. Destiny had a distinct memory of brownies being Luke's favorite treat when they were kids. Hopefully he still enjoyed them.

"Those sure smell good," Buzz said as he walked into the kitchen, sniffing the air in an exaggerated gesture.

"Hint taken. I put some aside for you on the stove," Destiny said, watching as her grandfather headed right over to the plate.

"You look nice," Buzz said through a mouthful of brownie. "And these brownies are out of this world."

"Thank you," she said, hoping she'd hit the right note between dressy and casual with her outfit. She was wearing a new pair of jeans with a red cardigan over a white tee and dangly earrings. She didn't usually wear much makeup, but she'd stained her lips lightly with a nice crimson shade. "I'm about to head over to Luke's place," she told him. "I fixed a plate for your supper. It's in the fridge."

"Good," Buzz said with a nod. "Nice to see you putting yourself out there."

Her grandfather's words rang in her ears as she made the drive over to Luke's. Putting herself out there with Luke was nerve-racking as well as exciting. But if she didn't step out on a limb of faith, there was zero chance of anything wonderful happening. And she wanted it all...the butterflies in her stomach, the tender kisses and the feeling that she was soaring.

When she arrived at Luke's home, it seemed to Destiny as if the entire place was lit up like it was Christmas. He had twinkling lights lining the walkway, and the entire house was glowing from within. She had a warm feeling just being here.

Luke flung the wooden door wide-open before she even had the opportunity to knock. "You're here," he said, ushering her inside from the cold. "Come in."

"Don't mind if I do," she said, clinging to her brownie pan as she hustled inside. The wind was so strong it practically blew her into Luke's home.

He closed the door and turned toward her. "Let me get your coat. You really didn't need to bring anything."

She wiggled her eyebrows. "You might change your mind when you see what I brought."

Luke took the pan with one hand and then helped her out of her parka with the other. "Why don't we head into the kitchen. Dinner's just about ready."

Destiny kicked off her snowy boots and placed them on the mat by the front door. Then she followed Luke into the kitchen, where he hung her jacket on the back of a hardwood chair before placing the pan on his marble counter.

"Do I smell brownies?" he asked, bending over and sniffing the aluminum foil.

"You sure do," she said. "Now what do I smell cooking?" she asked. A savory aroma filled the room, although she couldn't quite place the smell.

"Corn and crab chowder is on the stove and I'm baking some sourdough bread. I'm also going to make a salad with all the fixings." Luke sounded pretty pleased with his menu and she had the impression he didn't entertain very much. That made this dinner all the more special.

"That sounds delicious. Let me help with the salad," she offered.

While the food finished cooking, Destiny and Luke made the salad together, filling it with cucumbers, tomatoes, feta cheese and shredded carrots. Luke had already set the table, placing a bouquet of purple lupines in a vase by the place settings.

This was such a sweet and intimate atmosphere, one that smacked of something more than friendship. As they sat down to share the meal Luke had prepared, Destiny knew that the moment was approaching for her to peel back the layers she'd built around herself. She truly believed that this would be a bridge to creating a true and lasting bond with Luke.

Lord, please give me the courage to see this through. I want this to bring Luke and me together.

After clearing the table and filling the dishwasher, she and Luke settled in his living room to eat dessert. All of a sudden there was a huge lump sitting in her throat that wouldn't go away. She picked at her brownie, only managing to nibble a few bites. She could tell by the way Luke was darting glances at her that he'd noticed.

"Everything okay?" Luke asked. "Are you too full for dessert?"

"A bit. Your meal was terrific." She began twisting her fingers around. "Honestly, I'm just summoning the courage to tell you something. It's difficult to get the words out."

Luke leaned toward her, his expression intense. "Whatever it is, I've got you, Destiny. You can tell me anything and everything, just as I told you what I've been struggling with."

Her palms were moist as she began to speak. "Three years ago I went on a girls' trip to Nashville with a few friends of mine. While I was there I met someone. He came across as a good guy. He really seemed to like me, which was flattering. Being from a small town, sometimes you feel as if you've known everyone your whole life." Luke was listening to her so attentively she wasn't even certain if he was breathing. He was holding her hand, which felt really comforting.

She bit her lip. "He wanted to take me out while I was there." Waves of dark hair swung about her shoulders as she shook her head. "I should have said no, but I didn't. Why didn't I?" she asked in a low voice. "I was with my friends and that should have been my focus."

"Destiny, it's okay that you went out with him," Luke said, gripping her hand tighter.

"Going out that one night with Ned changed everything," Destiny said, letting out a little cry of despair.

"Take your time," Luke encouraged. "I'm not going anywhere. I'm right here with you."

She drew in a ragged breath. "We went out to dinner and then line dancing at one of those famous places in Nashville. It was really fun…until it wasn't. He wanted me to go back to his apartment, and I said that I couldn't. He kept pressing me and became really angry when I wouldn't budge." The more she spoke the choppier her breathing became.

"And then what happened?" Luke asked in a steady voice. She had the feeling he might know where her story was going but wanted to remain calm.

"H-he said that he would take me back to the hotel, but he wouldn't let me out of the car. I'll never forget the sound of that car door locking." She covered her face with her hands. Her entire body began to tremble.

Destiny felt Luke's hands removing her own from her face. He leaned over and began placing kisses on her tears. "It's okay. You don't have to hide from me."

She locked gazes with Luke, gaining courage from the way he was looking at her. His eyes exuded compassion. "That's not the worst part. H-he assaulted me."

The words sounded like a rocket going off to her ears.

Tears misted in Luke's eyes and he winced. "Destiny, I'm so sorry that happened to you. I know how awful that must have been for you."

"For a long time I struggled to stop taking ownership of what he did. I've gotten better with it, but it's been difficult. As you know, when something bad happens we tend to blame ourselves first. Why did I go out with him? Was it something I was wearing? Something I said or did?"

Luke placed his thumb on her chin. "It wasn't your fault. You didn't do anything to make it happen. He was to blame entirely."

"It wasn't my fault. I remind myself of that every day," she said. "And I wish that I'd had the wherewithal to file charges against him. But I didn't. I couldn't even manage to tell my friends because the shame ran so deep." She wiped tears away from her cheeks. "So I just flew home the next day and acted as if nothing had happened."

"That's understandable. You were on autopilot even though you must have been shattered."

"Yes, that's exactly it," she said, buoyed by his compassion. "At that moment I had to just put one foot in front of the other in order to survive."

Relief swept through her. Luke understood why she hadn't reported the assault. So many people struggled to comprehend why people didn't report attacks. It wasn't as straightforward as reporting it and prosecuting. So much more was involved that would have brought her to her knees. In a perfect world Destiny would have gotten justice, but that hadn't been the case. She'd learned to live with it.

"I came back home and only told Charlie, then a while later my friend Poppy. No one else knows."

He furrowed his brows. "Not your parents or Buzz? They seem as if they would be a great source of support." He was still holding her hand and tenderly caressing the skin.

"How could I lay that heavy burden on them? Buzz was dealing with my grandmother being sick, and my parents would have been beside themselves. I just couldn't do it."

"I totally get that. Telling my parents about Rico and Tony was hard enough. To this day they can't wrap their heads around my PTSD diagnosis, nor do they understand why I'm struggling to get back to my former self." He let out a brittle laugh. "There was no way I could explain that I've been blaming myself for their deaths."

"Not everyone will understand us, but I think it's pretty cool that we're on the same wavelength. We both have battle scars."

"But guess what? We're still standing. There's still fight left in us," Luke said. "Neither one of us gave in to despair. Before the explosion, I put my faith on the back burner." He made a face. "I'm not proud to admit that, but it's true. Ever since the explosion, God has been my rock."

Knowing Luke was a man of faith endeared him even

more to her. In her opinion he checked off all the boxes of how a man should be. Kind. Brave. Compassionate. Loyal.

"I don't know what I would have done if He hadn't been a huge part of my life," Destiny said. How many times had she cried out in the night, asking for relief from her pain? How many nights had she fallen to her knees and prayed for healing? Too many to count.

"I'm so grateful that you think so highly of me that you would share something so personal. I don't take that lightly."

She couldn't bottle up these feelings for another minute longer. He had to know that there was a very special reason she'd confided in him.

"I've grown to care a lot for you over the past few months. As more than a friend." The words tumbled off her lips. She leaned over and placed a kiss on his lips, one that hinted of all of her hopes and dreams about the future.

Destiny could only hope that he returned her feelings.

Luke's heart was pounding wildly in his chest after hearing Destiny's heartfelt words. Having her make the first move and plant a kiss on him was surprising and out-of-this-world amazing at the same time. Her lips were so soft and supple as they moved over his. A sweet floral scent clung to her and filled his nostrils.

As the kiss ended, Luke sighed and pulled away from her. He hadn't wanted this special moment to end. He would have continued kissing her until all the stars were stamped from the sky.

"You sure know how to surprise a guy," Luke said with a low chuckle.

"Hopefully in a good way," she said, her eyes wide. She seemed nervous, and all he wanted to do was allay her fears.

He reached out and pushed a few stray hairs away from her face. Luke wanted to see her expression at this exact moment. "In the best way," he confirmed. "Destiny, what you said about us being more than friends... I think we both know it's been moving in that direction. Whenever we're together I feel something between us. And as you said, it's a lot deeper than friendship."

She was listening to him intently.

"I think you're incredible in every way imaginable. What you revealed to me tonight just shows that you're strong and way more powerful than you realize. You remind me of a Sitka spruce—beautiful and majestic. They make it through the worst storms and emerge better than ever." He placed a kiss on her temple. "That's you, Destiny."

"Hearing you say that means the world to me," she said. "It was terrifying talking about my past, but you gave me a soft place to fall, Luke. I won't ever forget that."

"And I won't ever forget how encouraging you've been to me. We're both on a journey toward healing, so supporting one another is the most natural thing in the world."

"That's one of the reasons we understand each other so well."

Little had either of them known that their individual journeys mirrored one another's. He believed that they'd been drawn together like magnets for that reason.

"And because of the assault...that's why you decided to work with service dogs and help others?" The realization had just hit Luke like a wave crashing over him.

"Yes, it is," she admitted. "After the assault I also suffered from PTSD...anxiety, stress and flashbacks. I joined a program and was matched with a service dog. Olive. She changed my life in every way imaginable. She was a border collie who went everywhere with me." A little smile played around her lips. "She was everything to me. Helper. Companion. Faithful friend."

"Sounds a lot like Java," Luke said. He'd come to count on and adore the loyal husky more than he had ever dreamed possible, and Java wasn't even with him 24-7 yet. From the sounds of it, Destiny had real life experience with her very own service dog.

Destiny nodded. "They share a lot of the same attributes."

"I've never seen her with you or around the property," Luke said, looking at her curiously.

"I lost her quite suddenly. Have you ever heard of stomach flipping in dogs?" she asked.

"It sounds slightly familiar, but I don't really know what it is," Luke said.

"It's a gastrointestinal issue that comes on very quickly with dogs where their stomachs fill with gas or food, sometimes fluid, then twists. By the time I took Olive in to our vet, it was too late." The look of anguish etched on her face gutted Luke. She had been through so much—it just didn't seem fair.

"Oh, Destiny. I'm so sorry for your loss. I can't imagine losing Java at this point, so I know it must have really hurt."

"It did," Destiny said. "I was completely lost for a long time, but then a few things struck me. Olive came into my life for a reason. And that was to give of herself unselfishly and wholeheartedly. She walked me through some really dark times. Because of her, I came through the worst moments of my life. I recovered. Does that mean I don't ever struggle with what happened?" She shook her head fiercely. "No, it doesn't. But I am so much better now, thanks to the experience of being Olive's partner. I no longer need a service dog, but I'll never forget what Olive did for me."

"Also, my experience inspired me to help others who are in need of service dogs. For whatever reason under the sun. Anxiety. Epilepsy. High blood sugar. My goal was to lend a helping hand to those in need. To pay it forward."

"Which you've done spectacularly," Luke said, feeling incredibly in awe of this amazing woman. Was there anything she couldn't do? People called him a hero all the time, but she was truly a profile in courage and giving to others.

"That's sweet of you to say," she murmured. "And very much appreciated."

He caressed her cheek with his palm. "I speak the truth. I'm not sure you have any idea how wonderful you are."

A companionable silence settled over them, where neither needed to say a single word to fill the silence. He'd never had anything like this in his romantic life, this easy flow that was as natural as the sun rising in the morning. Destiny placed her head on his shoulder and they sat like this for a while.

"I really should be heading home, since I have early clients in the morning," Destiny told him.

"I understand. You're a woman on a mission."

Destiny's tinkling laughter filled the air. "What can I say? I'm determined to solve all the world's problems, one service dog at a time."

He loved her joyful laugh, enjoyed seeing her happy. Even after all she had been through, she shimmered. Destiny brought him contentment in ways he couldn't even adequately describe. He couldn't process the fact that he could be worthy of her affection.

"If you have any inclination to work with service dogs, there will always be a place for you at my K9 farm," Destiny told him. "Just giving you something to think about."

Luke felt a bit awestruck by her generous offer. "I appreciate that," he said. Although he appreciated Destiny's kindness, he wasn't sure if it would be a good idea.

"Thanks for a wonderful evening," Destiny said as she stood at his front door. "And for listening with such compassion."

Luke dipped his head and swept a good night kiss on her lips. "Get home safely," he whispered, holding the door open and watching her as she stepped up into the truck. A few moments later she took off down the road, red tail-lights blazing in the dark.

Everything seemed as if it was coming together like the pieces of a jigsaw puzzle. Yet he couldn't ignore the gnawing feeling in his gut that warned him that things were never this simple in his life. Something always happened to push him off course. He had a tendency to second-guess himself since the explosion, always questioning his worth.

Luke prayed that this time would be different.

Chapter Thirteen

"And then what happened?" Poppy asked, leaning across the table and waiting with bated breath for Destiny to respond. They were having dinner at Northern Lights and chatting up a storm. Destiny had been filling her best friend in on her dinner date with Luke. Just spilling the details out loud made her want to pinch herself to make sure she hadn't been dreaming. Luke had feelings for her!

All was right with her world. That was what love did to a person. Although she hadn't exchanged words of love with Luke, they were on the same page about having strong feelings for one another and pursuing a relationship.

"We kissed and talked about our feelings," Destiny said, resulting in a high-pitched squeal from Poppy. She clapped her hands over her face and giggled.

Poppy fanned her face. "Oh wow. You and Luke are on your way to being the town's most adorable couple."

"I don't want to get ahead of myself," Destiny said. In her experience, that was when things fell apart. And she so wanted to be in a relationship with Luke, to grow with him and see where things would lead.

"You're absolutely not," Poppy said. "It's perfectly normal to be excited and hopeful. You totally deserve to be adored."

A little sigh slipped past her lips. "It's pretty amazing how life works. Falling for my childhood friend who happens to be Charlie's bestie all while being his service dog trainer." She chuckled.

Poppy nodded her head knowingly. "From what I'm hearing, you're off to a great start. And it sounds like Buzz approves, which is icing on the cake."

Destiny laughed at how invested her grandfather was in her blossoming romance with Luke. She hesitated even thinking of their relationship in those terms since they hadn't made things official. It wasn't as if he was calling her his girlfriend.

Sean Hines, the owner of the restaurant and a popular figure in town, walked over to their table. "Whatever you're discussing must be mind-blowing," he said, chuckling. "The two of you have had your heads together since you sat down."

"We're having a grand time," Poppy said.

"Glad to hear it," Sean said. "Your food will be out in no time."

"Can't wait to taste the halibut," Destiny said, rubbing her hands together. "I'm on a fresh fish kick these days."

Thankfully, Serenity Peak was a huge fishing port with many local fishermen who made their living on boats.

"It's a good thing you live in Serenity Peak then," Poppy teased.

"Judah and his crew supply all of our fish, so you know it's the best," Sean agreed. Judah Campbell was a local fisherman who was also co-owner of Northern Lights. Not too long ago he'd married his childhood sweetheart, Autumn, with whom he was now raising a family in Serenity Peak.

"Let me know if you need anything," Sean said before walking over to another table.

"In case I haven't said it, I'm thrilled for you. No one deserves happiness more than you do." She reached across the table and gripped Destiny's hand in her own.

"Unless it's you of course," she responded. Poppy was such a warm and sincere person. She deserved love as well. Although her friend's romantic past had been full of deception, Destiny prayed she would be open to finding love.

Just then a group of men came into the restaurant—Luke, Charlie, Ryan, Brody and Caden. Destiny's heart leaped at the sight of Luke, who she hadn't seen in days. She had been so busy preparing for the showcase that they'd only managed a few texts here and there. One message had been very important. Destiny had texted Luke about the possibility of working at the K9 farm with her. She'd explained that adding a veteran to her operation would be beneficial to the program. Now that he was here at the diner, Destiny hoped they could discuss her proposition face-to-face.

Luke and Charlie spotted her at the same time, and although Luke's face lit up at first, his body language seemed a bit uncomfortable. Had she pushed too far with her suggestion that he join forces with her program? Charlie immediately came over to their table to greet them while Luke hung back.

Poppy looked over at the men's table and waved. She turned back to face Destiny. "What's up with Luke? Why didn't he come over?"

Destiny shrugged. "I'm not sure." She didn't want to make a big deal of it, but the fact that he hadn't come over with Charlie nagged at her. They'd admitted they had feelings for each other. At this point she wanted to tell Charlie that she and Luke were involved. She didn't feel right about keeping things from her brother, especially since he was tight with Luke and he had asked her at the festival if something was going on between them. Not clueing him in felt like lying.

Destiny wasn't used to keeping secrets from Charlie. Even as kids, they'd shared everything—the good, the bad and the ugly.

A few minutes later their dinner platters arrived—halibut with rosemary potatoes for Destiny and King crab legs and coleslaw for Poppy. A bowl of sourdough biscuits was also placed in front of them. Although the food was delicious, Destiny wasn't all that hungry. She found herself darting glances in Luke's direction. Her heart sank when he didn't meet her gaze.

What was going on? Had she crossed a line with him by suggesting they work together? She began racking her brain to uncover what was going on with Luke. Even his body language was odd—stiff and abnormal.

"You look upset. Maybe he's just having an off day," Poppy said. "It happens."

Destiny nodded. "Perhaps it's the setting. He isn't used to going out in groups. I think this might be his first time out at a restaurant since he's been home."

"There you go," Poppy said. "Shake it off. Don't let it ruin things."

"Of course," she murmured, trying to act unbothered, even though it was the furthest thing from the truth. She was saying words and making excuses for Luke, but Destiny wasn't sure she believed what she was telling Poppy. She hadn't seen Luke for days and had barely heard from him since dinner at his place. A lot of her emotions were tied into the fact that she'd never been in love before and even getting to a place where she could allow herself to fall had been difficult.

It was nerve-racking to think that she was going to have the rug pulled out from underneath her. Had things ended with Luke before they'd barely begun?

"We're way overdue for a night out," Charlie said, looking around the table. His gaze swung toward Luke. "You're being here is the cherry on the sundae. It's like old times."

They had all been in school together, growing up in a small Alaskan town and becoming a tight-knit group of friends. These guys were practically family.

"That's for sure," Brody said, his animated features showcasing his pleasure.

"Great to have you back home," Ryan chimed in. "We missed you."

It felt nice to be given the royal treatment by his friends. All four of them were outstanding men of good character. He was fortunate to call them friends. They hadn't seen each other often during his years as a SEAL, but they had the type of friendship that endured long absences. Catching up with one another was always festive and fun.

"You guys are the best," Luke said. "The last year has been pretty brutal, but things are starting to get better. Hopefully I'll be around a lot more."

"Amen to that," Caden said at the same time as his twin brother and the whole table erupted into laughter.

"Okay, time to focus on the menu before our waitress comes over," Brody said, turning his attention to the menu.

Luke tried not to stress out over the fact that Destiny was

sitting three tables away from him with Doc Poppy. All he really wanted to do was walk over and sit down beside her, forgetting everyone else in the establishment. He had been thinking of nothing but her for the past few days. And then her text had come across his screen, presenting him with a difficult dilemma. Being considered by Destiny as an asset to her K9 farm was mind-blowing and such a huge compliment, but it scared him to death. Working with Destiny would be an amazing opportunity to be of service to the Serenity Peak community, but it could also be disastrous if he fell apart at the seams. All this time he'd been wondering about what he could do with his life moving forward, and miraculously, Destiny had given him a road map. What he wouldn't give to feel strong enough to accept her offer. But he didn't feel worthy of the opportunity.

How he wished that he could get back to that idyllic place they had been in the night Destiny had been at his house. They had been on such solid ground. But once Destiny left and headed home that evening, doubts had begun to fester in Luke's mind. He'd leaned into all of his romantic feelings for her instead of taking a wiser approach. Should he have backed off? Heeded Charlie's advice not to let her down? He'd seen Destiny's vulnerability up close and personal with his own eyes. Despite her strength, she still had cracks that could break wide-open. And it gutted him to think that he could be the one to let her down and crush her spirit. The K9 farm was her pride and joy. How could he commit to working alongside her when he still wasn't whole? He'd experienced so many ups and downs over the past year, with no sign of things leveling off. He didn't trust himself to be the type of solid and dependable business partner Destiny deserved.

I'm worried you'll hurt her. Charlie's words sent a chill through him. In the cold light of day, he'd been worried about that too. It was all going around and around in his head until he couldn't think straight.

By the time the waitress came over and took their orders, Luke had a pounding headache. He ordered a cheeseburger and rosemary fries, picking something simple he didn't have to deliberate over.

"So, tell me about how you and Skye got together," he said to Ryan, looking for a little distraction from Destiny's presence mere feet away. Skye Drummond had always been beautiful and sweet. The last he'd heard, she'd been engaged to another man they'd grown up with. It just showed how quickly things could change.

"Do you want the short version or the one that involves the baby Skye found on the porch of Sugar's Place?" Ryan asked.

"I think the long version," he said, shaking his head. "Sounds like I missed a lot while I was deployed."

Over their meal they caught up on goings-on in their lives, and he surprised himself by disclosing details about the explosion and the deaths of Tony and Rico, as well as his trauma. They were all compassionate and thoughtful with their questions, which made the situation more comfortable than he'd expected. He was finding that the more he talked about his PTSD, the easier it became to bring it out in the open.

"We need to make this a regular thing," Charlie suggested. "Once a month at least."

"I'm in," Luke said. He could use the social interaction at this stage of his journey. Tonight had been progress, and if he didn't feel such a strain about Destiny, he probably would have enjoyed himself more.

They ended up leaving at the same time as Destiny and Poppy. As they all headed outside and said their goodbyes, he heard Destiny calling out to him. "Luke! Wait up."

He turned toward her, wishing he could avoid this encounter. Too much was building up inside of him, and it didn't have anywhere to go but outward. No doubt she'd noticed him being standoffish and wondered what was going on with him.

"Is something wrong? You barely said a word to me inside."

He clenched his teeth so hard he thought they might shatter. Of course she'd noticed how he'd basically given her the brush-off in there. Charlie's words kept ringing through his head.

Better to hurt her now than shatter her heart down the road. Or disappoint her with his inability to get his act together.

He wanted to feel worthy of loving this courageous woman, but he was afraid that he wasn't. Wasn't that what Charlie and Luke's ex, Brenda, had alluded to? And he was terrified of bringing hurt and heartache into her world. Hadn't she been put through enough? Pain ricocheted through his body.

How could he risk breaking her heart?

"I've just got a lot on my mind," he said. He wanted so badly to take her in his arms and soothe away her worries. But he couldn't get all of the warnings out of his head.

I'm worried you'll hurt her.

You've got too much baggage.

He couldn't be completely sure that he wouldn't hurt

Destiny. The very idea of doing so terrified him. Best to step aside and let her pursue a relationship with someone who was whole and emotionally healthy. As much as he wanted it to be so, that just wasn't him. Maybe it never would be.

"Anything you want to talk about?" Destiny asked, folding her arms around her middle.

He seemed so detached, his expression shuttered. She barely recognized him. Right before her eyes he'd transformed back into the Luke she'd seen the first day he had shown up at her K9 farm. He had erected a wall around himself that seemed impenetrable.

Had she done something to cause this?

"Nothing I can think of," he said in a curt tone. "I'm good."

"Luke, you can tell me anything. Remember?" she asked in a soft voice.

"I think you should focus on the showcase instead of me. That's what is important. It's in two days."

That's what he was thinking about? The showcase! She would much rather talk about the two of them and why he was acting so distant.

"B-but what about us? I thought we were—" She moved toward him, grasping his arm.

He took a step back, causing her to suck in a steadying breath. His body language spoke volumes. And it wasn't anything good.

He looked away from her. "I'm sorry, but I don't think we should ruin a friendship by pushing for more. We've always been good friends. Why run the risk of messing things up?" A tortured expression sat on his face.

"And we can still be," she sputtered. "They don't cancel each other out. Both things are still possible."

"I—I'm not sure of that," he muttered.

"Why?" she asked, unable to mask her confusion. "Why are you saying this?"

He let out a low groan. "We both have healing to do. Do you really think we'd be good together? It's kind of a long shot." He let out a brittle laugh that sounded like nails on a chalkboard. "And I haven't exactly been winning lately."

She swallowed past the bile in her throat. "I was willing to try," she said. "The other night you were all in. What's changed?"

He finally looked at her with flat eyes. Where had Luke gone? For the first time it hit her that maybe she didn't know him at all. He opened his mouth but no words came out.

She understood. He didn't want to crush her by telling her that he just didn't have strong feelings for her. It was written all over his face. No words were necessary.

Her lips quivered and she willed herself not to cry. *Please please, don't cry in front of him!* "I can't expect you to feel something you don't feel. 'Night, Luke."

She needed to leave before every ounce of her pride evaporated. Destiny couldn't understand this abrupt turnabout in his intentions. She couldn't help but wonder if it was because of what she'd revealed to him about her assault. At the time he'd been compassionate and supportive, but perhaps once he'd thought the situation over, it had been too much for him to deal with along with all of his own issues.

Destiny didn't want to think it was true because it was soul crushing. She'd believed in him and the possibility of them, only to have it all vanish in a puff of smoke. The pain was unbearable.

When she was alone in her truck, Destiny finally allowed the tears to fall as she watched Luke drive away. She cried hot, salty tears that caused her stomach to hurt. She hadn't cried like this in years. She wasn't mad at Luke. How could she be? He was still the most wonderful man she'd ever known. Just because she was in love with him didn't guarantee that he would love her back. She had always known that simple fact. And he hadn't strung her along either. His words had been straightforward and to the point.

But she hadn't anticipated things ending so abruptly or the way her heart would shatter into a million jagged pieces. She hadn't known it would be such a lonely, gutting feeling.

How long would she feel this way? Because at the moment it seemed like it might just be for a lifetime.

Chapter Fourteen

Luke woke up feeling as if he had been run over by a semi-truck. He was hurting now, aching in a way he never had. It was completely different than the way he'd grieved after the explosion, but it was grief nevertheless. After leaving Destiny at Northern Lights, Luke had felt as if his heart had been split wide-open. There was no cure for this type of heartache. His only option was to push through it.

All this time he'd been hoping to build something lasting with Destiny, even though he'd always known she was out of his league. And he had lit a match to their relationship the other night, all in an attempt to spare her further hurt down the road.

There weren't many things in this life that were perfect. But she was. She was also vulnerable. Charlie had warned him for that very reason. He knew his sister had been through a lot. Luke had seen up close and personal how traumatized she'd been. And he was still broken. Still searching for a way to put all his broken pieces together. Destiny couldn't count on him to be an equal partner in any way, shape or form. He would only disappoint her and cause her further damage.

He loved Destiny. Truly. Deeply. And with every fiber of his being. The realization had swept over him last night with painful intensity. He wouldn't hurt this much if he didn't love her. Putting the brakes on what they had been building had brought him to his knees. She was at the center of the world he'd been creating for himself, right along with his spirited service dog. He didn't know what he would do without Destiny in his life. And how could she be in his life now? After the showcase, his service training would be over, and Java would be living with him full-time. For all intents and purposes, their connection would be severed.

But loving someone meant protecting them, didn't it? Even if it was from himself.

The question remained…had he done the right thing? Or had he just caved and allowed the opinions of others to get in his head? Either way, he'd allowed the best thing in his life to slip through his fingers.

With nothing but time on his hands, Luke decided to do something he had been putting off. He sat down with his computer and began writing an email to Mrs. Martinez. It was time. He might not have the perfect words, but he was going to try his best.

Dear Mrs. Martinez,

I hope that you're doing well. Or as well as you can be under these sad circumstances. For me, the past year has been filled with grief, shock, loss and guilt. First, let me tell you that Rico was one of the bravest and most compassionate souls I've ever known. He taught me a lot about friendship, life and his beloved Shakespeare plays. He talked about his family all of the time, so much so that I felt that I knew all of you.

With regards to the explosion, everything happened

so fast. I sincerely don't think him or Tony suffered. I have missing pieces of my memory, but I do know that for certain. I've dealt with a lot of guilt, wondering why I survived and they didn't. I'll probably never know the answer to that, but I'm determined to live a life worthy of all three of us.

Rico wasn't just a SEAL hero. He was a hero in life.

Blessings,
Luke Adams

When he was done, Luke heaved a tremendous sigh. He dug out a box of cereal from his cupboard, then shook some cornflakes into a bowl before pouring oat milk over it. Luke slumped down into a chair and began going through the motions of eating breakfast. The cereal was bland, which served as a metaphor for his life at the moment. All of the brilliant colors in his life were now washed-out and gray. How long would this feeling last? Something told him it might persist for a lifetime.

He bent his head in prayer. All he kept thinking about was the Bible verse from Psalms 30:5. *Weeping may continue for a night, but joy cometh in the morning.*

Where was his joy? He had arisen the past two mornings feeling just as untethered as he had last evening.

All of a sudden his front door burst open. He could see Rosie standing in the doorway from where he was sitting at his kitchen table. She was leaning heavily on her cane.

"Don't stand on ceremony. Just come inside why don't you?" he asked curtly. It bugged him that she'd just barged in without knocking. Maybe he was just cranky.

She walked into the kitchen with a sheepish expression

stamped on her face. "You haven't been answering your phone. I was worried."

In an instant, all of his annoyed feelings toward Rosie dissipated. Despite her own health challenges, she was always looking out for him. "Sorry. I—I'm a bit on edge," he told her. His phone was charging and he hadn't been checking his messages.

"I can see that. What's wrong? How did things go last night?" she asked, sitting down his across from him.

He made a face. "Dinner with the guys went well, but… Destiny was there with Poppy."

Rosie smiled. "A happy coincidence, right?"

Luke quirked his mouth. Just thinking about their encounter filled him with shame. "Not really. I know you guessed something was brewing between us, but… I kind of put on the brakes." Just saying the words out loud made him feel stupid. He ran a shaky hand across his stubbly jaw. Luke hadn't shaved in days, and he knew he looked a mess.

She leaned toward him. "Now why would you go and do a foolish thing like that?"

He pushed his bowl of cereal away from him, sickened by the sight of his mushy meal.

"It's complicated," he answered. "She's been through a lot…things that would rob most people of their faith and rock them to their core." He shook his head. "I can't say any more." Although he loved and trusted his sister, there was no way he could violate Destiny's privacy.

"You don't have to break any confidences. Life can be cruel." Rosie's voice exuded wisdom. She knew a lot about life not being fair. It sometimes seemed to him that Rosie had been fighting uphill battles her entire life.

"I'm still a work in progress. I just felt so much doubt

about being able to shield her from more heartache," he confessed. "I didn't want her to get hurt again. Or let her down."

"Whatever made you think that you would hurt her?" She gripped his hand. He couldn't help but notice that her motor skills were weakening. Yet Rosie was always so brave and determined to forge ahead without complaining.

For a moment he wrestled with whether or not to tell her about what Charlie had said to him. He had a gut feeling that Rosie wouldn't like it one bit.

Luke steepled his hands in front of him. "Charlie told me to tread lightly with Destiny. He said he was afraid that I was going to hurt her, let her down."

"Charlie said what?" Rosie exploded. "That's outrageous. How dare he interfere in your relationship?"

"Easy there, tiger. He's being a protective older sibling, which you should understand better than anyone." They both knew that Rosie had done many things in the past to protect Luke. "You would do the same for me under similar circumstances, wouldn't you?"

She frowned. "I suppose so, although I don't like tearing couples apart."

"It wasn't all his fault. I never told you, but my ex, Brenda, really did a number on me. She dumped me after my PTSD diagnosis, and her exact quote was that I had too much baggage. Maybe she was right."

"She wasn't!" Rosie hissed. "Sounds like a true narcissist."

Thankfully his ex-girlfriend lived in Boston, otherwise he would be afraid of Rosie confronting her. She was loyal to her core.

"I can't argue with you on that point," he responded.

Rosie made a fretful sound. "But where are all of the doubts coming from now? You've been doing so well."

"Everything kind of piled up," he admitted. "I truly believed that she would be better off without me. Destiny is one in a million. It's hard to fathom that I deserve her."

"Of course you do, Luke. But you've got to start believing it. Hey, it's obvious you love the woman." Rosie looked him straight in the eye, her gaze like a heat-seeking missile.

"I—I." He was floundering.

"Did I stutter? You love her," Rosie repeated, as if it was an established fact.

"For so long I haven't considered myself worthy," he said.

"You *are* worthy of all the good things this world has to offer."

His shoulders heaved. He hadn't yet said those three humongous words out loud. "I do love her," he said, confirming what his sister already seemed to know. "I really do, Rosie. She's everything to me." Now it was real. The words hung in the air, crackling like fireworks.

She scoffed. "So what are you going to do about it? Sit here and eat your Wheaties?"

"I'm supposed to be attending the showcase today as well as graduating from the service training program and bringing my girl Java home." He bit the inside of his cheek. "I don't even know if I should attend the showcase after what went down between us."

"Luke! You can't let Destiny down like that. She's counting on you to represent her and the K9 farm. Not to mention the fact that I need an in with her. I've been thinking a lot about doing the service training myself and getting my own dog."

"That's a fantastic idea, sis," Luke said. Both of them knew that Rosie's condition was a debilitating one. The ravages of MS could be brutal on one's body. A service dog like Java would definitely improve her quality of life.

She smiled at him. "You've been a source of inspiration, little brother. Please don't lose sight of the fact that you've done so much good in this world. I'm proud of you."

His eyes burned with unshed tears. Hearing this right now from his big sister was just what he'd needed to put things in perspective. "Thanks for lifting me up. You're right about everything," he said with a nod. "I'm going to fight, not just for Destiny, but for myself as well. And Java," he added.

"So what you're saying is that you're in love with both Destiny and Java? Is that what I'm hearing?" Rosie asked.

Luke let out a huge laugh that rolled through his body like a clap of thunder. It felt good to be in such high spirits. Talking things over with his big sister had been just what he'd needed to turn his thinking around.

No one could stop him from loving Destiny. He'd lost sight of that in one awful moment of self-doubt. The powerful love he harbored for her wouldn't allow him to hurt her. How could he not have realized that before now? Doubt was the enemy and he had been blinded by fear.

Suddenly, he was filled with hope. Maybe he hadn't totally blown it with the woman he loved. There was only one way to find out. By showing up at the showcase and letting her know in no uncertain terms that he wanted and needed her in his life. He needed to make things right.

He wanted her to be his. For keeps.

The morning of the showcase, Destiny had to drag herself out of bed. The aroma of bacon and eggs wafted into her bedroom. Buzz, understanding that she was dealing with heartache, had insisted that she sleep in this morning to get some extra rest before the showcase. Little did her grandfather know that she had tossed and turned the past few nights, unable to get thoughts of Luke out of her head. Although she'd been looking forward to the showcase for months, Destiny now dreaded it. Would Luke show up, she wondered? If not, it would break her heart all over again. And if he did, things might get awkward between them.

"Come in," she called out in response to a knock on her bedroom door. Charlie was standing there with a bouquet of flowers in his hand.

"Hey! What are you doing here so early?"

"I got a call from Pops, so I swung by to make him breakfast."

She let out a snort. "You? Cooking? Am I in *The Twilight Zone*?"

Charlie pressed his hand against his chest. "Ouch! That hurts." He handed her the flowers in the vase. "These are for you. Congratulations on the showcase. You've worked so hard to build your business and make a difference for others."

"Oh, Charlie. Hearing you say that means the world to me, especially now." Receiving flowers from someone she loved when she was feeling so low was uplifting. Earlier, she hadn't been sure that she could go through with the showcase, but now she knew that it was a must. As the saying goes, the show must go on.

"So fess up. You didn't just swing by to make Buzz breakfast." She had a good idea that her grandfather had spilled the details of her situation with Luke.

Charlie nodded. "He told me about you and Luke. Not

that you ever told me that anything was going on, but I suspected."

"To be honest, things were building over time. We got very close, and before I knew it, I fell for him."

"I suspected that the two of you were involved. And I need to apologize," he said, shifting from one foot to the other.

"Apologize? For what?" Destiny asked. "I'm the one who kept you in the dark."

Charlie grimaced. "I spoke to Luke the day of your show-case practice. I warned him off you."

Goose bumps popped up on the back of her neck. "What? Charlie! What did you say to him?" She was starting to break out in a sweat.

"I told him to be careful with you," he admitted. "And that I was worried he might hurt you."

Destiny was shaking with anger. "I—I can't believe you did that. You put doubts in his mind about us. And you took away my choices as if I'm a child who needs to be watched over. That wasn't your place to interfere."

He held up his hands. "I know what I've done, especially since Pops told me about what happened between you and Luke. Please know that I was only trying to protect you."

"Charlie, that may have been your intention, but I'm a grown woman. You can't put me in bubble wrap for the rest of my life."

He ran a hand over his face. "I know. It's just that what happened to you—"

"Exactly. It happened to *me,* not you. I'm the one who lives with it, who deals with the anxiety from it and who has worked really hard to move past the assault. I deserve love. I deserve to be able to choose who to love." Her breathing was choppy as she spit the words out. She couldn't ever remember being so angry in her life. Now, the pieces of the puzzle were coming together. It had been so confusing to witness Luke's complete turnabout, but Charlie had gotten in his head and made him believe that he wasn't good for her. There were other factors too, including the pressures of reintegrating into society and the job offer she'd made. For Luke, it had all been too much.

"What can I do now to fix things? Should I go to his place and talk to him?" Charlie asked. "Tell me how to help."

"For starters, you should just butt out," a raspy voice said from the hallway. "Stick to making breakfast instead of butting into other people's personal lives."

"Amen!" Destiny said. "I don't want you to do a single thing. The only person who's going to talk to Luke about this is me."

Destiny prayed that Luke showed up today for the showcase. It would provide her with the perfect opportunity to tell him that she knew why he'd been so dismissive the other night. He hadn't meant a word of it. She was inwardly rejoicing. All this time her gut instinct had told her that Luke's feelings matched her own. She wasn't wrong.

Today, one way or the other, she was going to get Luke to admit that his feelings for her were as deep as Kachemak Bay.

At twelve o'clock sharp Luke drove up to Destiny's K9 farm. Once he got out of his truck, he noticed several other vehicles and a bunch of Destiny's clients gathered around. The showcase wasn't starting for another hour, so Luke knew he had a little bit of time to find Destiny and get Java ready to strut her stuff.

He made a beeline to the barn, hoping to see Destiny there. If not, he would head up to the house and find her there. It might be a little awkward if Buzz was there. He and Destiny were close, and he imagined she'd confided in him about their situation. Buzz might just have written him off.

She was standing with Isaac, placing bows on each of the canines. The moment he stepped inside Java spotted him, and although she was being obedient and lying down, Luke could tell by her wagging tail that she wanted to run to his side.

Just then Destiny noticed him, and he watched as she told Isaac something that caused him to take all of the pups—minus Java—outside. As he walked past him, Isaac flashed him a thumbs-up sign, a gesture of silent encouragement he appreciated.

Luke walked toward Destiny at the same time as she moved in his direction. They both stopped when they were within a few inches of one another. She'd swept her hair up into a high ponytail. Dressed in a burgundy parka and black leggings, she looked sporty and as beautiful as ever. Slight shadows rested under her eyes, and he couldn't help but think she had endured a few sleepless nights like him.

"Luke. You're here. I wasn't sure you were going to show up." Destiny sounded surprised.

"I wouldn't miss this for the world."

"The other night—" she began.

He reached out and placed his finger across her lips. "The other night I acted like a fool," he admitted. "I allowed fear to overshadow my true feelings."

"Because of what Charlie said to you?"

"He told you?" Luke asked, feeling a bit incredulous. He hadn't expected Charlie to come clean about their conversation.

A frown marred her face. "Yes, and his ears might still be ringing. I let him have it."

"Why doesn't that surprise me," he said, trying to keep a straight face. He would have loved to have seen her in action. Even as a kid she'd been feisty and no-nonsense.

"No one has the right to try to decide the course of my life. Not even you, Luke."

He scratched his jaw. "I didn't think that's what I was doing. It wasn't just what Charlie said to me. I've been dealing with self-doubt for a long time," he admitted. "The idea of letting you down has been gnawing at me. I know how much the showcase means to you, as well as this K9 farm. I convinced myself that I would make a mess out of everything, even the job you offered me."

"I'm sorry if I put too much pressure on you. That was never my intention," Destiny said, sighing. "I know you were trying to protect me, but in doing so, you took away all of my choices. You made a decision to turn away from me to avoid the risk of hurting me, but you didn't give me any agency in the decision."

He hadn't even thought about that aspect. But she was right. He'd made a decision based on his own fears without even giving her a chance to share her feelings.

"I'm sorry, Destiny. That was the furthest thing from my mind."

She took a step closer toward him. "I choose to love you, Luke. And nothing or no one is going to convince me otherwise."

His jaw dropped. "You love me?" he asked, shock ringing out in his voice.

"I do, Luke. And I'm not afraid to shout it from the rooftops." She was grinning now and looking up at him with such pure joy that it made his stomach do somersaults.

He reached down and placed both hands on either side of her face, looking deeply into her eyes. "I came here to tell you that I'm head over heels in love with you, but you've beaten me to the punch. I'm madly in love with you, Destiny." He dipped his head down and placed his lips on hers, sealing his declaration with a kiss.

When he pulled away, Luke saw tears shimmering in her eyes.

"I hoped that you felt the same way as I do, but hearing you say it is more wonderful than I ever could have imagined. After the other night I almost gave up hope."

Causing her pain was the very thing he had been trying to avoid. Yet, by doing the noble thing, Luke had wounded her.

"For a while there I even wondered if you were pulling away from me because of what happened in Nashville," she confessed. "On some level I knew that couldn't be true, but it did cross my mind a few times. And it hurt."

His heart sank. Why hadn't he considered that she might make that awful connection between her disclosure and him putting the brakes on things? It was the furthest thing from the truth, but under the circumstances, he didn't blame her for believing it.

"Oh, sweetheart, hearing that is gut-wrenching. Let me tell you that I would never back away from our relationship for that reason." He gripped her hand, linking it with his own. "What happened to you wasn't your fault. It doesn't define or limit you in any way, shape or form."

"Thanks for putting that out there," Destiny said. "It matters to me."

"I'm so sorry that I put you through all this, Destiny. Sometimes we do foolish things, all in the name of love."

"I forgive you," she said, lacing her arms around his neck. "I think when people are in love, things can happen to cause one another pain. It's how we recover from those moments that's important."

"I promise you that I'll spend the rest of my life trying to make it up to you," he vowed. Luke's sentiment hung in the air between them like a promise.

"What are you saying?" she asked, suddenly seeming nervous.

"What I'm saying is that I don't want to walk through this life alone." He reached for her hand. "And what I feel for you, Destiny, tells me that I want you to be by my side for a lifetime."

She blinked away tears. "I feel the same way. We've known each other all our lives, so it's only fitting that we continue on this path, right?"

He smoothed back a few stray strands of her hair. "Who would've thought that I would fall in love with Charlie's little sister?"

"And who would have thought that I would fall in love with the boy from down the road who always fought my battles for me? Swoon," Destiny said, placing her hand over her heart.

Luke couldn't help but feel that the past had always been there, serving as a bridge to their future. Meant to be, almost as if their love story had been written in the stars.

"I don't have a ring or anything yet, but I hope I'm making my intentions clear. Destiny, I want you to be my other half."

"You had me at I love you," she said, laughing and wiping away tears from her cheeks. "Everything else will fall into place. I just know it."

"I truly believe that too." And he did. His heart was full in a way that completely surprised him. He'd never imagined his very own happily ever after, simply because he hadn't believed he deserved one. His mindset was different now. He was going to grab hold of happiness as tightly as he could. "I found out the hard way that tomorrow isn't promised. We have to cram as much joy into today as possible."

"Amen," Destiny said. "And that starts today."

She looked at her watch. "I've got to line everybody up for the showcase. I can see guests are arriving."

Luke rubbed his hands together. "Let's get this show on the road." He turned toward Java, who was still lying peacefully as she'd been instructed. "Come on, Java," Luke said, beckoning her to his side. The Husky raced over and sat beside Luke, looking up at him with adoration.

"Are you ready to bring Java home after this?" She shook her head at Luke and Java. "You've sure got this girl wrapped around your finger."

"Which girl? You or Java?" Luke asked playfully, encircling her waist with his hands and drawing her against his chest.

Destiny swatted at him and chuckled. "Let's go. I can't wait to see you strut your stuff."

Destiny, Luke and Java walked out of the barn into the Alaskan sunlight. The sky was a perfect shade of cornflower blue with barely a cloud in sight. Luke reached for

Destiny's hand and joined it with his own. He still had healing to do, but Luke knew that if he kept doing the work and putting one foot in front of the other, he would continue to make progress.

From this point forward, he planned to put the pieces in place to create a life with this incredible woman. With love on their side, he knew they would soar to amazing heights.

Epilogue

Luke knew with a deep certainty that everything that had happened over the past year and a half had been building toward this moment. He didn't have a nervous bone in his body about marrying his best friend and the woman of his dreams. His heart was bursting with gratitude.

Lord, thank You for this day and this amazing woman of faith. I know You had a big role in our journey. Please watch over us as we embark on this new life.

Destiny had shown him that he was stronger than he'd ever known. She had given him the world and a bright, shiny future. He now knew that he could move past the fear and the misplaced feelings of guilt. He hoped that he'd given her just as much in return. A love for all time. A person to lean on when the storms of life passed through.

He was on his way to being whole again. And even if he never got back to one hundred percent, he knew Destiny would continue loving him. And he would love her till his last breath. They had both been through the fire, and due to their love for one another, had made it through to the other side. God was good.

Footsteps echoed on the flooring, pulling him from his thoughts.

"How are you holding up?" Charlie asked, playfully slapping him on the back. He was decked out in his finest suit as best man.

"Amazingly well." Luke held out his hand. "See? I'm as steady as an arrow. Not shaking at all."

"Cool as a cucumber." Charlie chuckled. "The two of you were meant to be. It couldn't be any more perfect."

"She's my destiny," Luke quipped, trying to keep a straight face as he delivered the line.

Charlie groaned. "Oh, that's bad."

Luke chuckled along with his soon-to-be brother-in-law.

"What did I miss?" Caden asked as he entered the room.

"An incredibly corny joke," Charlie said, rolling his eyes. "A real stinker."

"No time for jokes. It's time to get this show on the road," Caden said, looking at his watch. "You've got a date at the altar with the woman of your dreams."

"You don't have to tell me twice," Luke said. He beat a fast path to the door, eager to make it to the altar, where he would soon meet his stunning bride.

Serenity Church was filled to the rafters. Everyone had come out to show them their support. It meant the world to him to see so many townsfolk giving them their blessing. Being part of a community was such an important thing, which he'd discovered over the course of the past few months.

With Charlie and Caden at his side, Luke stood at the altar as the strains of "Here Comes the Bride" filled the church. Java trotted down the aisle, with the ring pillow clenched in her teeth. As always, she was classy and solid, performing her ring bearer duties with distinction.

When Destiny made her appearance right after Poppy and Rosie walked down the aisle, Luke immediately teared up. She was breathtakingly beautiful in her white silk and taffeta gown, an heirloom piece from her grandmother, Junie.

How, he wondered, had his life taken such a beautiful turn? Coming home to Serenity Peak had turned everything around and given him love everlasting.

"I thought we said no tears," Destiny whispered once she reached his side.

"I'm not tearing up," he said. "There's just something in my eye."

Destiny chuckled. "What a coincidence. I've got something in mine too." She swiped at the tears on her cheeks and took a deep breath. This was the day all of her dreams were coming true. She was becoming one with the most courageous, selfless man she'd ever known. They had both endured many dark nights of the soul, yet now their happiness was overflowing. Psalm 126:5 came to mind. *They that sow in tears shall reap in joy.*

Luke reached for her hand and clasped it in his as the pastor began the ceremony. Destiny could hear several sniffles in the congregation as they recited their vows.

"Till death us do part," they said in unison, knowing they had many years to live out their dreams with one another. Java came forward at just the right time and stood beside them with the rings. It felt so right to have the husky there with them, since she had been such a big part of their love story. Luke got down on his haunches and untied the rings, then ruffled the top of Java's head. "We couldn't do this without you, Java girl."

Isaac stepped forward and brought Java back to his pew. She dutifully sat beside him.

Destiny and Luke shared their first kiss as man and wife

as the guests vigorously clapped. It was the sweetest kiss of all time, serving as a symbol of their union. "Forever," Destiny whispered against his lips.

"Come what may," Luke said. "In good times and in bad."

"Thank you for always defending me," Destiny said, sweeping her palm against his cheek. "Because of you, I feel safe and loved. And not judged as I feared that I would be."

"Right back atcha, beautiful. You made me feel worthy at my lowest moments. You gave me the courage to put myself out there."

"I'll always fight for you," Destiny said. "And for us."

As they walked through the church doors and outside into the sunlight, they were showered with birdseed and shouts of congratulations. Everything had worked out so perfectly, from her wedding dress to Java being in the bridal party.

"I've been meaning to ask you something," Luke said, studying her face. "I never really responded to your offer about partnering up in your K9 business." He smiled down at her. "Are you still looking for a partnership?" Luke knew with a deep certainty that this would be a great path for him going forward.

Destiny tapped a finger to her chin. "Hmm. A partner? I'm not so sure about that. They would have to be pretty good with dogs," she teased.

"Check," Luke said. "They're really good with canines."

"The person would have to be a hard worker."

"Check." Luke made a motion with his hand as if checking something off a list. "They work like a dog." Destiny rolled her eyes and groaned.

"And lastly, they would have to be absolutely devoted to the owner."

"That's the easiest one of all," Luke said, grinning. "Double check."

"Well then, they're hired."

Luke let out a whoop of excitement then lifted his wife in his arms and spun her around.

"Let me down. I'm getting dizzy," she cried, laughing good-naturedly. Luke quickly complied, setting her down on the ground.

"How did we get here, Mr. Adams?" she asked, looking around her at all the guests who had shown up for them today.

"With a lot of love and belief in one another, Mrs. Adams," Luke answered before dipping his head and pressing a tender kiss on Destiny's lips.

They both knew that today was just the beginning of their beautiful love story. Together they had weathered the storms of life. With faith and love, all things were possible.

* * * * *

*If you enjoyed this story
by Belle Calhoune,
Check out other stories in the
charming Serenity Peak series,
including the latest*
His Secret Alaskan Family
Available now from Love Inspired!

Discover more on LoveInspired.com

Dear Reader,

Thank you so much for joining me on another Serenity Peak book. I hope you enjoyed Luke's and Destiny's journey to finding love. This is a very emotional story, as it involves trauma sustained by both the hero and the heroine. I often thought that they were mirrors of one another due to their emotional trauma, although their individual situations are quite different. With faith and courage, both characters fight to get their lives back, as well as their happy ending.

And let's not forget about Java. She's such a faithful, spirited companion for Luke as he works toward healing and getting back what he's lost. This sweet service dog is the heart of the story and a hero just like Luke.

Healing is the theme of this novel. Luke and Destiny each help the other with their individual healing, which is a beautiful thing. They provide each other with a listening ear and a soft place to fall. No judgment. Just love. It's a great ingredient for a relationship and provides a strong foundation for their future.

I love writing for Harlequin Love Inspired. Working in my pajamas is an amazing perk of the job. It's a wonderful feeling to be able to reach readers with an inspirational romance and an uplifting message. I enjoy hearing from readers via my Facebook Belle Calhoune author page and via email at scalhoune@gmail.com. Until next time!

Blessings,
Belle Calhoune